S0-BUA-900

QUACKY AND THE HAUNTED AMUSEMENT PARK

CHILDREN'S BOOKS BY WALTER OLEKSY

If I'm Lost How Come I Found You?
Quacky and the Crazy Curve Ball
Careers in the Animal Kingdom
Laugh, Clown, Cry
The Universe Is Within You
Women in Men's Jobs
Treasures of the Land
*The Green Children and Other Outer Space
   Aliens*
The Golden Goat
The Road Runners
Undersea Adventures
The Black Plague

Walter Oleksy

QUACKY AND THE HAUNTED AMUSEMENT PARK

McGRAW-HILL BOOK COMPANY

New York   St. Louis   San Francisco
Montreal   Toronto

06105676

DEL ROBLE SCHOOL LIBRARY

To Scott Kingdon, Rusty Burge,
Bill Ward, Scott and Greg Jones,
and Scott, Dick and Josh Hambrook

All characters in this book are fictitious. Any
resemblance to persons living or dead is coincidental.

Copyright © 1982 by Walter Oleksy. All Rights
Reserved. Printed in the United States of America.
Except as permitted under the Copyright Act of 1976,
no part of this publication may be reproduced
or distributed in any form or by any means, or stored
in a data base or retrieval system, without the prior
written permission of the publisher.

1 2 3 4 5 6 7 8 9 M U M U 8 7 6 5 4 3 2 1

LIBRARY OF CONGRESS CATALOGING IN PUBLICATION DATA

Oleksy, Walter G., 1930–
Quacky and the haunted amusement park.
Summary: When his dog Puddles becomes the victim of
dognappers, Quacky pursues his only clue: the sound
of a dog barking in an abandoned amusement park.
[1. Mystery and detective stories. 2. Dogs—Fiction.
3. Amusement parks—Fiction. 4. Orphans—Fiction]
I. Title.
PZ7.045383Qu   [Fic]   81-12338
ISBN 0-07-047753-1   AACR2

CONTENTS

1. "HAPPY BIRTHDAY,   1
   DEAR PUDDLES!"
2. SPOOKY BUSINESS   14
3. SMART LIKE A FOX   23
4. OLD FOLKS AT HOME   38
5. THE CALL OF THE WILD   54
6. A MAN'S BARK   63
7. QUACKY TO THE RESCUE!   76
8. GOING FOR THE BAIT   87
9. MATTIE'S LUCK   96
10. A NEW TRAP IS SET   114
11. SPOOKS ON THE LOOSE   128
12. DOORWAYS TO MYSTERY   138
13. UNDER A FULL MOON   150
14. ONE LAST STRAY   161

1

"HAPPY BIRTHDAY, DEAR PUDDLES!"

"Have you seen Puddles?" Quacky asked Aunt Maggie. "I've searched everywhere inside and outside the house for over an hour."

"He hasn't been in the kitchen all afternoon," she replied absently while spreading white icing on a chocolate layer cake she had baked. "I told you that the last time you asked." Aunt Maggie's gray hair was liberally tinted blue and she wore a lacy party dress that had been fashionable in the 1930s. It hung on her long, thin frame like an old curtain, Quacky thought.

Quacky, short and lean, was freshly scrubbed, but he was wearing his oldest blue jeans and an old green Army surplus shirt he had found at the bottom of a box at the Salvation Army store. It still displayed a corporal's yellow stripes on the arm. His long, straight, blond hair hung down over his ears, and his usually bright eyes were troubled.

"You'd think he'd be wagging his tail around here, looking for his birthday presents," he muttered unhappily.

Quacky wasn't sure of Puddles's age, or his dog's birthdate. Like Quacky, he was an orphan. Aunt Maggie was Quacky's mother's aunt. He had never known his parents.

Quacky figured that Puddles, a dark brown Labrador retriever with one white paw and a white streak on his neck, was just about full grown. His size meant he was now about a year old and deserving of a birthday.

In honor of the occasion, Quacky had decided to throw a little birthday party, and Aunt Maggie had baked the cake in Puddles's colors. But now the guest of honor was missing!

"I'm sure he'll turn up soon." Aunt Maggie looked up from the cake. "He's probably over at Mattie Mayflower's. Haven't you been saying that Puddles found a girlfriend in her dog, Patricia?"

They stared at each other. Quacky was glad his aunt didn't put into words what was worrying him. Dognappers were on the prowl in Smedley. Mostly they were taking wealthy people's dogs and demanding ransom for their return. But Quacky was worried even though neither he nor Aunt Maggie had much money. He was afraid the dognappers might have stolen Puddles by mistake.

"I suppose Puddles is at Pattie's." Quacky's voice still sounded troubled. "But when I looked in Miss Mayflower's yard a while ago, I didn't see either dog."

Puddles and Pattie were the same color and had the same markings. They were identical as twins, except for one thing.

"Did you go up and ring her doorbell and ask if Puddles was there?" Aunt Maggie stopped icing the cake and glanced impatiently at him. He knew why. It was because she knew *that* would be the last thing Quacky would do.

Mattie Mayflower, a lady even older than Aunt Maggie, lived in a large, gray stone house on a big wooded lot up the block. A high iron fence surrounded the property. It was a spooky place, Quacky thought. He wondered how Puddles could like going there. Even if his girlfriend did live there. Quacky had never seen anyone but Miss Mayflower enter her house, not a milkman, not even the mailman.

The postman always slipped mail under the gate. It stayed there until dark. Quacky had noticed that the mail was always gone in the morning. He figured the old lady picked it up on her way to or from the all-night grocery store two blocks away. She never came out of her house during the daytime, and, as far as he could tell, she came out at night only to get the mail and go grocery-shopping.

"Do you think Miss Mayflower is very rich?" Quacky was still reluctant to get any closer to the house than the gate, but he wondered about the old woman who lived beyond it.

"The Mayflower family always was rich," Aunt Maggie recalled, piling cookies on a plate. "They were one of the wealthiest and oldest families in Smedley. Mattie's the last of them. Most people think she's still rich, but just stingy, hoarding all her money. But lots of folks in town, me included, wonder just how well off she is now, her place looks so run-down."

Aunt Maggie's explanation did not relieve Quacky's mind any. Most people believed Mattie Mayflower was rich, and her dog Pattie looked just like Puddles, except that she was a female. Maybe the dognappers had stolen Puddles, thinking he was Pattie!

"Go ahead and ask Mattie if Puddles is there," Aunt Maggie urged him, hurrying to set the cookies on the dining-room table.

Quacky followed her. "Can't you just phone her and ask?"

"I tried to telephone her once, but she doesn't have a telephone. See how stingy she is? Won't even spend money to have a tele-phone in the house. Go on now, Quacky." She gave him a push and went back to the kitchen. "It's getting late, and a rainstorm is coming. We've got to have this party pretty soon."

The doorbell rang.

"The guests are here already!" Aunt Maggie exclaimed. She was upset because she wasn't ready for them yet.

Quacky went to the front door. Ralph Dooley, the police chief's son from next door, a round, bookish-looking boy with black-rimmed glasses and braces on his teeth, stood on the doorstep trying to control his giant-sized dog, Clemontis Regis, a black-and-white spotted Dalmatian. Clemontis was straining at her leather leash and barking excitedly at the other animal guests being carried up the walk by their masters.

Tennis Harper, a tall, thin boy with short blond hair, in painter's bibbed overalls, held a small, square, wire cage with a hamster inside. Will Kelly, a short boy who seemed all black hair and buck teeth, brought a long, striped king snake in a similar cage. Katie Nolan, the last of the group, held a dome-shaped birdcage with a yellow parrot inside. A tall girl in baseball pants and sweatshirt, she wore her long red hair in pigtails.

The parrot was squawking and Clemontis Regis was barking. The hamster was chittering and the snake hissing.

"Where's Puddles?" Tennis asked over the

din as Quacky led them all inside to the parlor.

"He's on the prowl somewhere," Quacky replied, trying not to look as worried as he felt. "He'll be here any minute. You guys see him outside on your way here?"

None of his friends had seen the dog.

"Oh dear!" Aunt Maggie stood in the foyer and wailed at the sight of the pets. "I knew I'd regret allowing a menagerie to the party!" She looked in the parlor. "Now, Ralph, you'll have to get Clemontis off my couch."

Quacky's Uncle Otis, a distinguished-looking old man in a black suit with vest, was trying to watch television, but the huge dog nearly sat on him.

"Take this beast off me!" Uncle Otis shouted as Clemontis Regis tried to lick his face.

Ralph pulled his dog off the couch and then chased after her as she barked and bounded through the parlor and into the dining room, where Katie was standing near the table, holding her parrot.

"Polly want a cracker!" Katie Nolan's parrot began squawking over and over. The bird was flapping its wings wildly in the cage, frightened by Clemontis, who was sniffing at it.

"I've been trying to train Oscar to say something special," Katie confided to Quacky. "But, so far, he hasn't learned it. He has sort of a limited vocabulary."

"Polly want a cracker!" the parrot squawked

again and again until Katie finally got him to shut up.

Will Kelly had his king snake out of its cage, and it began coiling itself around his neck.

"Oh, my heavens!" Aunt Maggie nearly dropped the cake she had brought to the dining-room table, which was all set up with paper birthday plates and cups and favors. "Put that snake back in its cage before it bites us all!" she exclaimed nervously.

Will laughed. "He's harmless, Aunt Maggie." But he unwound it from his neck and put it back inside its cage.

"We can't have a birthday party without Puddles, can we?" Quacky looked desperately at Aunt Maggie just as loud rumbles of thunder were heard.

"Well, go out and look again, one last time," she told him impatiently. "But be back in no more than ten minutes, because that's when I start scooping the ice cream onto the plates. And, Quacky, I didn't expect a snake!"

Tennis Harper volunteered to help Quacky; he placed his hamster cage on his chair at the table.

Quacky and Tennis left the house and began walking north up the block as a strong wind blew up. Storm clouds gathered overhead, and lightning split the darkened sky. It was still afternoon, but the late fall thunderstorm was turning the sky as dark as night, and dead

leaves began blowing around in the strong
wind.

Standing before the high iron gates of the
Mayflower property, the boys could hardly see
the house in the shadows of the trees and
bushes. Just then, lightning flashed, and the
house was illuminated for an instant; then it
was swallowed up again in darkness.

"This place gives me the willies." Tennis's
voice cracked as he spoke. "It's almost as
spooky as Riverland, the old abandoned
amusement park south of town. I've been sort
of hanging around there lately, and, if you ask
me, it's haunted!"

Normally Quacky would have picked up on
that and asked Tennis more, but right now his
mind was on finding Puddles.

"There's a spot somewhere along here where
Puddles gets through. A couple of bars are
missing in the fence."

Finally he found the opening, some distance
to the left of the main gate.

"You're not going to crawl through there, are
you?" Tennis asked anxiously.

"I'm just going to call to Puddles from here,"
Quacky explained. He was glad Tennis seemed
as scared as he was about entering the property. "He's come out through here the other
times I've called."

But this time Puddles did not come running

through the opening in the fence when Quacky
called for him again and again.

"I sure wish Jerry was home," Quacky confided. "He'd go ring Miss Mayflower's doorbell
and get Puddles for me. But he's working late
at the mortuary." All Quacky's friends knew
Jerry. He boarded with Aunt Maggie. But he
was more a friend than a boarder. "Jerry's
learned how to embalm bodies."

"That's all I had to hear!" Tennis cried, pulling Quacky by an arm. "Let's get out of here!"

Quacky let himself be half dragged away
from the fence. Thunder roared, lightning
streaked, and the wind began blowing harder.

"Puddles is afraid of lightning."

"Don't tell, but so am I!" Tennis admitted.

Soon the boys were running as fast as they
could, back to Aunt Maggie's.

The party went on without the birthday dog.
Quacky sat unhappily at the dining-room table
with his friends and their pets. Uncle Otis
reluctantly joined them.

Quacky thought his Uncle Otis looked ridic-
ulous. He was all dressed up in his business
suit, with a cone-shaped party hat perched on
his head. But Quacky was still too worried
about Puddles's absence to smile.

Tennis had brought a little bag with a few
green beans for his hamster. Katie Nolan gave
her parrot some seeds.

But Aunt Maggie would not permit the king
snake to be on the table. Will Kelly kept his
pet in its cage, on his lap.

Clemontis Regis was busy on the floor beside
Ralph, chewing on a liver-flavored plastic
bone. Quacky almost laughed at that, because
he knew Puddles was too smart to be fooled by
a plastic bone. No matter how hard he tried to
be a good host, his thoughts kept drifting back
to Puddles.

"And what did you bring for your pet?"
Uncle Otis asked Will mischievously.

Aunt Maggie set dishes of ice cream in front
of Tennis and Quacky and sat down, giving her
full attention to Will Kelly.

"What *do* king snakes eat?" she asked.

Will's buck teeth showed prominently in his
wide grin. "Chameleons, frogs, and live rats."

"Oh, my, no!" Aunt Maggie gasped, pushing
her chair away from the table.

"Don't worry, I fed him at home before I
came," Will assured her.

Slightly relieved, Aunt Maggie began lighting
up the five candles on Puddles's birthday cake.

Quacky knew they had to go ahead with the
party, even though Puddles wasn't with them.
Aunt Maggie had gone through a lot of fuss,
and everyone had come over with their pets,
and it was going to rain any minute. They had
better get the party over with soon, so his
guests could avoid the storm.

"Why five candles?" Quacky asked as Aunt Maggie lit the last of them. "Puddles is only one year old."

"One candle's too easy to blow out, after you make a wish," Aunt Maggie explained. "So I figured I'd put five candles on the cake, one for each pet at the party. Puddles temporarily excluded."

The friends liked that. Quacky kind of liked it, too. It seemed somehow less lonesome to him, especially when he thought of them singing "Happy Birthday."

Aunt Maggie asked Otis to turn out the lights over the table, and when he returned to his seat in the darkened room, she began the singing.

"Happy birthday to you. Happy birthday to you. Happy birthday, dear Puddles. Happy birthday to you!"

"Happy birthday, Puddles!" Katie Nolan's parrot squawked just as Quacky blew out the candles.

"That's what I was teaching him, but that's the first time he ever said it!" Katie exclaimed.

Quacky didn't tell them, but his wish was that Puddles would come back home right away.

After the cake, cookies, and ice cream, Aunt Maggie took up her banjo and began singing a song new to Quacky: "He May Be an Old Dog in an Old Town, but He's a New Dog to Me!"

As they laughed and clapped, they heard the front door slam and Jerry call out:

"Hey, anybody want a wet dog?"

Quacky and his friends looked at Jerry in surprise as he came into the dining room. He was followed by a dog whose dark, soaking fur was plastered to his body.

"Puddles!" Quacky cried, pushing away from the table and running to hug the dog, getting all wet in the process. "Where have you been?"

"I found him scratching on the front door," explained Jerry as he took off his dripping raincoat. He was a tall, strong-looking young man, and his face and dark hair were wet. "Guess you couldn't hear him crying outside, with all the singing and the thunder and rain."

"You're home early," Aunt Maggie said as she got up from the table. "Thought you were going to work late tonight at the mortuary?"

"I told Nick Stitch I didn't mind embalming in the daylight, but even *I* get a little scared embalming after dark, in a thunderstorm!"

Aunt Maggie got a towel and as Quacky began drying off the wet dog he looked at Jerry. Jerry wasn't afraid to admit he was afraid, when he was. It was one of the things Quacky liked best about him.

His friends crowded around as Quacky continued to rub the dog, when suddenly he exclaimed:

"Hey, wait a minute! This isn't Puddles. It's *Pattie!*"

"Happy Birthday, Puddles!" the parrot squawked.

094293

2

SPOOKY BUSINESS

With Pattie's surprise arrival, the party ended. Uncle Otis was enlisted into driving the guests and their pets home, in Aunt Maggie's old red Volkswagen bug, crowded as it became.

Ralph ran home next door with Clemontis Regis.

Since the wet dog that had come home was not Puddles but Pattie, Aunt Maggie told Quacky he should take the dog to her rightful owner, Mattie Mayflower.

"She's probably as worried about Pattie's whereabouts as you've been about Puddles," Aunt Maggie told Quacky. "I know it's stormy and raining outside, but it's likely to keep up all night. So the sooner you take Pattie home, the better."

Quacky looked helplessly at Jerry.

"Okay, I'll go with you." Jerry relented though his shoes still sloshed with each step he took.

They both got into raincoats, and Quacky put a leash on Pattie. As they hurried through the rain, lightning flashed overhead, and the wind nearly blew them off their feet. But they managed to reach the front gate of Mattie May-flower's property.

"I guess I just can't escape spooky places tonight," Jerry admitted.

When Jerry tried the gate, it opened easily. Quacky was surprised. He had expected the gate to be locked with a chain or something.

"She hasn't been out yet tonight," Quacky observed, stooping down just inside the yard and picking up two envelopes. "Her mail is still here. It's soaking wet."

"Don't read them, just pick them up, and bring them along," Jerry told him, pulling Quacky along with Pattie.

They hurried on up a stone walkway that weeds and bushes were trying hard to cover. The wind blew wet leaves against their faces from the high hedges that lined the walk.

Finally they reached stone steps that led to a big, long, open stone porch. Even under the roof of the porch, the rain beat against them from the sides and back.

The big window next to the front door was

dark. "I don't see any lights on inside," Quacky whispered hoarsely.

"Maybe the storm blew out her lights. Ring the bell."

Quacky looked at Jerry and hesitated.

"Go ahead, or we're going to drown out here," Jerry persisted.

Quacky never thought he would actually find himself standing in front of Miss Mayflower's front door on a dark and stormy night, ringing her doorbell.

He pressed the bell and waited. And waited.

"Maybe she's gone to bed already," Quacky suggested. "Let's come back in the morning."

Pattie began to whine. Quacky figured the dog was anxious to get inside the house.

"It's not eight o'clock yet," Jerry said. "I don't think she's gone to bed, not while her dog's not home. Ring it again."

Quacky pressed the bell button again, this time harder. They waited again, but still no one came to the door.

"Maybe the bell doesn't work." Jerry knocked on the door.

Quacky held Pattie's leash loosely. He felt sorry for the dog, which now was scratching on the door, whimpering.

The door slowly began to creak open.

Quacky hid behind Jerry and then peeked around him at a short, frail old lady in a raincoat and snowboots. A yellow rain hat of plastic flopped down almost over her eyes.

"We found your dog," Jerry told her just as she saw for herself. Pattie, beside herself with happiness, tried to jump up into her arms.

"I was just going to go out looking for her," the old lady gasped in a weak voice, hugging her wet pet. "I was so worried. She's been gone for hours. I'm sorry." She seemed suddenly to become aware of their wet clothes. "Won't you come in out of the rain? It's such a nasty night!"

Quacky reluctantly followed Jerry into a hallway. A musty odor came to his nose. The place smelled like the basement of a museum he had been in once, when he ran away from an orphans' home in New York City. *I'll bet she doesn't open the windows to let in fresh air,* he thought.

"You'll have to forgive me," she apologized. "I'm so happy to have Pattie back safely, I'm forgetting my manners. I'm Mattie Mayflower."

She shook hands with Jerry and then with Quacky as they introduced themselves.

"It's my dog, Puddles, that has been coming over lately to visit Pattie," Quacky told her. He still wasn't sure of the house and kept looking over his shoulder, expecting someone to sneak up on him.

"Oh, so that's who that dog is!" Miss Mayflower exclaimed. "Well, he can come over as often as he likes. Pattie seems to be quite taken with him, and so am I. He's a nice, gentle dog."

Most of the time, Quacky said under his breath.

"Is everything all right here?" Jerry asked, trying to peer beyond the dark hallway. A dim light was showing from a room on the other side. "Has the storm blown out your electricity?"

The old woman appeared apologetic or ashamed, Quacky was not sure which.

"I'm afraid I haven't had electricity in some time, young man," she admitted, stroking Pattie on the head as the dog leaned affectionately against her. "It's just too expensive. I have a kerosene lamp I take with me, from room to room."

So that's the light coming from the other end of the house, Quacky thought. An old kerosene lamp.

"Will you come in for some hot chocolate to warm you? I've some towels you can dry off with. Please don't go right away," she pleaded. "Tell me where you found Pattie."

They followed her through an almost empty house, past a big parlor, a dining room twice as big as Aunt Maggie's, and finally into a kitchen. Quacky noticed that there was almost no furniture in most of the rooms.

"I live here all alone, except for Pattie," she told them, handing each a towel she took from a kitchen closet. "And when Puddles visits. You should have brought him along tonight."

"I don't know where he is," Quacky replied as he dried his face off. "He's been missing since before the storm."

"Oh, I am sorry," she said sympathetically.

After taking off her rain togs, she began making hot chocolate at an old stove.

"It's probably the storm," she said. "It spooks some animals. He's probably warm and cozy, under some porch somewhere. I'm sure he'll turn up soon, just as Pattie has."

While Quacky and Jerry watched, she put some wood into the belly of the stove, and sparks flew. Jerry explained that he had found Pattie huddled outside Aunt Maggie's front door, wet from the rain.

"I don't know where she was before that," Jerry added. "Maybe she was with Puddles, and one of them got frightened from the storm, and they ran in separate directions."

Quacky was fascinated by the old wood stove. He had never seen one like it before. It wasn't the big, round, pot-belly type that Jerry had in his Fix-It Shop. This one was square and very big, though it was also made of black cast iron.

"I almost forgot. Here's your mail." Quacky

handed the old lady the two envelopes he had found just inside her gate. "You won't have to go out tonight."

There was a kind expression on her small, wrinkled face, as if she knew he was aware of her nightly excursions.

"Oh, I'm afraid I'll be going out anyway, in a little while."

They were curious to know why she would go out in such a rainstorm, even for groceries, but she did not explain.

"I don't like mail much," she confessed, accepting the envelopes from Quacky. They were both very wet. "I don't have anybody to write to me anymore. All I ever get are bills, or other bad news."

She peered first at an envelope that was blank on both sides.

"This one is odd. There's no writing on it. It isn't addressed to anybody, and there's no return address."

Puzzled, Quacky and Jerry watched as Miss Mayflower opened the blank envelope and read a note on a small sheet of white paper that was inside.

"This is strange," she said and held out the paper for them to read.

Quacky read it aloud:

"Dear Rich Lady—I've got your dog. It'll cost you $500 to get him back. *Cash!* I'll contact you later. *Don't call the cops!*"

"Oh, no!" Quacky cried, looking at Jerry. "They've got *Puddles!*"

When they got back home, they found a troubled Aunt Maggie.

"Otis has gone again!" she wailed. "I know he has!"

"But he went to drive the kids home," Jerry reminded her as he and Quacky took off their raincoats.

"I've called them all, and he took them all home, even Katie Nolan and her parrot out on the west side of town. But he should have been back by now."

"Maybe the car broke down," Quacky suggested lamely. "You know how it almost never runs when it rains."

"He'd have called for Jerry to come and help him." Aunt Maggie was sure. "He's run away again. Oh, he'll never come back now. He's got the car and can go a long way."

Quacky could see it wasn't losing the car that saddened her. It was losing Otis again. This was the second time he had run away since Quacky had been staying with Aunt Maggie. The man just didn't like being tied down to a family, Quacky suspected.

But Quacky had worries of his own. "The dognappers have Puddles!" Quacky explained the whole story to his Aunt Maggie. "What can I do?"

"All we can do tonight, I suppose, is phone the police."

"It's just raining too hard to go out and look for him anymore," she said glumly.

"We can't do that!" Quacky insisted. "Dog-nappers might take it out on Puddles, if we sic the cops on them."

Aunt Maggie tried to comfort Quacky with a hug, but he was too upset to be encouraged.

In bed later that night, as the storm cracked and rumbled, and the wind blew more violently than ever, Quacky lay wide awake. He missed Puddles fiercely and worried about him being held a hostage somewhere by dog-nappers.

Once or twice, before he finally fell off to sleep, Quacky thought he knew now how Aunt Maggie must be feeling. He had lost Puddles, and she had lost Otis. It wasn't any fun, he thought: losing the one you love.

3

SMART
LIKE A FOX

Something awakened Quacky in the dark early hours of the morning. Lightning was still striking, and rain was washing hard against the windows in his bedroom.

He could hear voices outside his room, and people walking around.

"Puddles is back!" he cried, leaping out of bed. He ran out into the hall in just his boxer shorts and saw Aunt Maggie and Jerry running around in their bathrobes and slippers, putting buckets under leaks in the ceiling.

"It's even worse in the attic!" Aunt Maggie told Quacky. "Hurry and get some more pots and pans from downstairs, and give us a hand."

He joined them in a frantic effort to catch some of the rainwater that was seeping through half a dozen or more places in the hallway ceiling and in some of the bedrooms.

"I thought I fixed the roof last spring," Jerry apologized.

Quacky and Aunt Maggie followed him back up to the attic, all of them carrying pots, pans, and buckets.

"I guess a patch-up job wasn't enough," Aunt Maggie explained. "I've needed a new roof for years. But it took a heavy rain like this to prove it."

They put the containers under as many dripping leaks as they could, and Aunt Maggie picked up a mop to swab the floor. The attic was separated into three rooms that she used as bedrooms when she had a lot of house guests or boarders. The ceilings were leaking in all three of the rooms, and the water that had collected on the floor soaked through to the ceilings of the rooms on the second floor.

When they finally had the pots and pans and buckets placed strategically, Aunt Maggie stopped and leaned on the handle of her mop.

"Well, I guess after all we still should be thankful we've got a roof over our heads, even if it does leak badly," she told them.

Quacky knew what she meant. Four of Aunt

Maggie's bridge-playing old friends were soon to be without a place to live.

"I think it's a terrible thing, to make condominiums out of so many apartment buildings," she complained. "My friends have lived in their building for almost twenty years. Now they get the bad news that it's going condo. But they're all too hard up to buy their apartments, so they have to move. And because so many buildings are going condo, rents in the rest of the rental buildings are going out of sight. I just don't know what they'll do!"

It was just like his Aunt Maggie, Quacky thought, to worry about somebody else's problems while she had such big concerns of her own, such as Uncle Otis splitting on her again and her roof about to cave in.

"By golly, I've got an idea!" she exclaimed, moving an old dented pot closer to catch a direct hit from a rain drip in one of the attic bedrooms. "I'll invite my friends to live here with us! They can have these attic rooms and I'll just charge them a little rent, something they can afford. The two men can have their own rooms and the two ladies can double up in this one; it's the biggest."

Quacky could see how Aunt Maggie's new idea was shaking her out of her own worries.

Maybe that's how to get over a loss, Quacky wondered. If you're worried about someone

OBSOLETE

you love who is gone, don't stew over it. Get busy doing something, especially something for somebody else.

Next morning when Quacky woke up, the first thing he did was run to the window and look out. He knew the rain had stopped and that the storm was over, because he didn't hear the thunder or lightning anymore, but he somehow hoped that if he looked out the window and down to the front yard, he would see Puddles there.

Puddles was not down below in the yard, but Quacky's eyes looked a little beyond to a red Volkswagen parked out in front of the house. He ran out of his room excitedly, calling to Aunt Maggie.

Before he got downstairs he saw her in her robe and hair up in curlers, with a pancake flapper in one hand.

"I know, I saw it when I got up a while ago," she sighed. "Otis brought the car back, but he must have done it during the night. He's still missing. For good this time, I've a hunch."

Quacky did not have to tell her how sorry he was. He knew she understood that he was.

He wanted to hurry out and look all over again for Puddles, and skip going to school. But Aunt Maggie insisted he eat some pancakes and have some milk first.

While he ate, or rather picked at his breakfast, he heard Jerry already working around the house, emptying full pans of rainwater and moving things around.

"Jerry told me about your visit with Mattie Mayflower last night," Aunt Maggie gossiped. "He said he offered to go to the store for her, if that's why she had to go out afterward, in such a storm. But she said she wasn't going shopping. I wonder why she would go out so late and in such terrible weather? He said she has almost no furniture and doesn't have electricity and cooks with an old wood stove. She sure holds on to her money, I'd say!"

Quacky's thoughts were on Puddles, and he hardly heard her.

"Oh, all right, Quacky!" Aunt Maggie finally relented. "I know you don't have much time before school. Go on and look for Puddles. But don't skip school today. You've been doing that a few too many times lately. And if you find those dognappers, let the police handle them, do you hear?"

Quacky ran out the back door and found Ralph in his backyard, playing with his dog. Clemontis Regis never could figure out how to catch a frisbee in his mouth, the way Puddles always caught one on the fly.

"Puddles come home yet?" Ralph asked.

"He's been dognapped!" Quacky told him and then explained. "I'm going out looking for him again. Want to come along?"

"I've still got a couple of math problems to do before school. You're not going to skip today, are you?"

"I guess I may cut a class or two," Quacky confided in a whisper, so Aunt Maggie would not hear.

"You'd better make Social Studies or Miss Effie's going to report you to the Principal," Ralph warned.

Social Studies was Quacky's last class of the afternoon and he always got very restless about then. If it was nice out, as it was today, he found it hard to resist cutting the class. All day long he would be looking out the windows of his classrooms, wishing he were outside playing with Puddles. By the time his two o'clock Social Studies class came around, he could hardly stand staying cooped up any longer.

"I'll be there," he told Ralph as he got on his bicycle. "But don't look for me any earlier, unless I find Puddles."

"Hope you find him!" Ralph called out as Quacky sped northward up the block.

When he reached Mattie Mayflower's, he stopped and got off his bike and leaned it against the fence. He didn't see her anywhere, but that didn't surprise him, since he had only seen the old lady leaving her house a few times before, and always at night. Come to think of it, he realized, he had never seen her going back into her house at night. He had only seen her leaving it.

I wonder why she did have to go out last night, after Jerry and I left her?, he thought to himself.

He didn't see Pattie outside either, and got back on his bike and headed farther north.

After having no luck in finding Puddles all morning, Quacky decided to take a chance and go over to the police station. He would not tip his hand and admit he was looking for his own lost dog, in case the dognappers might take it out on Puddles. But he thought he could maybe find out something there.

As he entered the station, Quacky saw two old men standing in front of the sergeant's desk, arguing about something. He recognized them as two of Aunt Maggie's senior citizen friends who sometimes came to the house to play bridge with her and her lady friends.

"They're my shoes he's got on!" one of the men was trying to convince the sergeant. "We're roommates, but he just thinks anything of mine is his as well."

"I bought these shoes to disco in, Sergeant," the other man broke in. "He's always claiming my stuff is his."

It surprised Quacky that either of them would be interested in disco-dancing, much less be able to do it, they looked so old. The man in the shiny black patent-leather disco shoes had long gray hair that needed trimming. He wore red slacks and a wrinkled plaid sport-coat that looked a little big on him.

The man who claimed the shoes were his was the same size, tall and thin, but he wore his gray hair neatly trimmed and had a thin gray mustache. He was better dressed, in gray slacks and a blue blazer that fit him better. But the shoes he had on were brown, old, and un-shined. Quacky figured the disco shoes proba-bly belonged to this man.

"Make him give me my shoes back!" the well-dressed man complained.

"He took my brown shoes, now he wants these, too!" the other man argued.

"Hey, look, fellas," the bear-sized sergeant growled. "I've got bigger fish to fry than two old guys arguing about a pair of shoes. You both get lost, you hear?, and don't bug me again. This is the hundredth time you two have come in here with some kind of complaint. Ei-ther get along, or don't be roommates any-more."

"We can't afford places of our own; the rent's too high," the man in the disco shoes complained.

"We've *got* to live together," the man with the mustache grumbled. "It's an economic ne-cessity."

"Then get along," the desk sergeant ordered them. "That's a *social* necessity. Now get out of here, and next time you guys come in here arguing about whose underwear the other one is wearing, I'm gonna run you *both* in!"

While the two old men began leaving the police station, Quacky looked after them and tried not to laugh.

"And what's your problem?" the sergeant asked Quacky.

"I just wondered," Quacky said hesitantly, turning to look at the sergeant. "If you caught the dognappers yet. And maybe some of the dognapped dogs got turned in this morning?"

"Is your dog missing too?" the sergeant asked, studying Quacky.

Quacky still thought it would be too risky, if he admitted that Puddles was dognapped, even if it was only by mistake. "No, I'm just asking, for a friend."

"I'm sorry, Sonny," the officer told him. "There must have been a dozen people asking about their lost dogs already today. The dognappers would have to be pretty busy, to get all those dogs. Most of the dogs probably aren't stolen. They're probably running around town lost, without their name tags. If people would just keep their dog's tags on, maybe we'd be able to find some of them."

But Quacky was sure Puddles had not just wandered off somewhere. He was being held a prisoner somewhere, for ransom.

"I've got some men investigating, but the

leads just aren't there," the officer explained. "Now why don't you and your friend just go out and look around again? Maybe you'll find the dog before we do." The sergeant began eyeing Quacky suspiciously. "Hey, shouldn't you be in school?"

Quacky left hastily, before the desk sergeant could try to sic anyone on him for cutting school.

Out of desperation, when two o'clock rolled around and he had still not found a trace of Puddles, Quacky rode his bike over to Mac-Dougall Elementary. The school had been named after the grandfather of Chester Mac-Dougall, president of the First National Bank of Smedley, Connecticut.

He would be a few minutes late, but that would come as no great surprise to his Social Studies teacher, Miss Irmgaard Effie. Even with such a screwy name, Quacky thought she was probably the prettiest teacher he had ever had. But that still didn't keep him from cutting her class often.

About to enter her room, he laughed to himself. It was what the police sergeant had told the two old men: it was just a matter of "social necessity" to Quacky that he cut his last class of the day so often. When it was nice outdoors, like it was that afternoon, he just had to get out. If Miss Effie's shocked out of her mind about anything, he figured, it would be that he was actually coming to her class that afternoon, instead of cutting it!

Miss Effie, a tall, slender woman with long brown hair, wearing a nice, light-green dress, was visibly surprised to see Quacky show up. His classmates whistled and clapped their hands as he came into the room, and Miss Effie pounded a ruler on her desk to restore order.

Quacky went to the back of the room and slouched into his regular seat at a desk in the last row, right behind Ralph. Ralph gave him a look that asked if he had found Puddles yet, but Quacky shook his head negatively.

Across the aisle from Ralph sat Tennis Harper. He was thirteen, a year older than Quacky and Ralph, but had fallen a year behind in school because he had been sick a lot one year. He had always minded that, until he came to MacDougall Elementary that fall. Quacky and Ralph liked Tennis and were glad they were in the same classes.

Seeing Tennis, Quacky remembered for the first time what Tennis had told him the night before, about Riverland, the old, now-abandoned amusement park that stood boarded up on the far south end of town. Once, long before Quacky was born and even before Aunt Maggie moved to Smedley, Riverland had been a big, gaudy, noisy, wonderful place with roller-coaster rides, fun houses, a midway with magicians and clowns, and popcorn, soda, and cotton candy. Now it was empty, deserted, and quiet as a graveyard.

But what's this about Riverland being haunted?, Quacky wondered. He leaned over and started to ask Tennis about it, but Miss Effie banged her ruler again and glared at Quacky from across the room.

"Now, class, I'm glad all of you are here today," she started to say, still glaring at Quacky. "I want all of you to take part in a new Social Studies project I've been working on."

Oh, great!, Quacky said to himself. She wants us all to clean up the gutters in Smedley, or empty everybody's garbage. Her idea of Social Studies, Quacky was beginning to believe, was for all of them to do some free clean-up work for the school or the city.

"Smedley is a very old town, one of the oldest in Connecticut," Miss Effie went on. "I think it would be a very meaningful class Social Studies project for each of you to report on something very old in Smedley. Like a landmark. First you will learn all you can about it, and then you will give a class report on it. Each of you will select a different project to work on."

It wasn't such a bad idea, Quacky told himself grudgingly, compared with most of her other ideas. He remembered the one he liked least, a few weeks back, when they all had to go to the city dump and see how the garbage was disposed of.

He liked old things. Like Aunt Maggie, he half laughed to himself. He even liked her old red Volkswagen, although it was always conking out and was especially temperamental in the rain. Now what old thing can I study in town?, he wondered.

His classmates immediately began raising their hands, anxious to ask Miss Effie permission to study the old things they had on their minds.

Several of the smarties in class got the first pick, Quacky noticed, because Miss Effie always answered their raised hands first. But they were taking the dumb and obvious things, he thought. Like the Smedley Public Library, which was in an old mansion that some rich family had left the city a hundred years ago or more. Another got to study the City Hall, which was even older.

Everything that's safe and right under their noses, Quacky sneered, disgusted with his classmates. Still, he couldn't think of a better or even less obvious old thing to study.

Everything in town that he could think of that was old was taken in just a few minutes. Quacky racked his brain and was about to

raise his hand and ask Miss Effie if he could report on *her*. But he figured she really wasn't
old enough to qualify.

Suddenly, a great idea came to him and
Quacky raised his hand excitedly. But Miss Effie recognized Ralph's raised hand first.

"I wonder, Miss Effie, if I can report on the
old Mayflower house?" he asked.

Darn!, Quacky said to himself. That's just
what *I* was going to pick!

"It's supposed to be one of the oldest houses
in Smedley, but I don't think anyone knows
much about it," Ralph explained. He didn't
look at Quacky, but Quacky got the idea that
Ralph knew he was stealing Quacky's choice of
old thing.

"Why, that's a very good idea, Ralph," Miss
Effie told him. "An unexpected choice. I wish
some others of you had chosen a less obvious
old place."

Quacky was really stumped now, without an
idea in his head, which wasn't like him at all.
His usually active imagination was failing him
now.

Finally, Miss Effie recognized Tennis, whose
hand had been the first to go up, but which
had been ignored the longest.

"I'd like to study something in town no one
else has picked yet, but I think it's so big, it
would have to be a two-man job," Tennis ex-

plained. He half turned in his seat and gave Quacky a quick look.

Quacky figured he knew what Tennis was up to now. It was a great idea! A stroke of genius!

"I'd like for Quacky and me both to study and report on Riverland, the old abandoned amusement park on the south end of Smedley," Tennis asked. "I guess it's been vacant for years, but it used to be just about the busiest place in town, with roller-coaster rides and magic shows and midway and ferris wheel and merry-go-round and all. And Aladdin's Castle is still there, a big spook-house."

"Why, that's a wonderful idea, Tennis," Miss Effie replied. "And I think you're right, about it being too big for one person to study. All right, you and Quacky can have that to report on."

Quacky leaned across the aisle, and he and Tennis shook hands on their deal.

"You old fox, you!" Quacky laughed.

"Fox, heck!" Tennis replied. "I'd be too *scared* to check out Riverland all by myself!"

4

OLD FOLKS AT HOME

After class, Quacky, Tennis, and Ralph met outside the school, and Quacky told Ralph he didn't really mind that Ralph picked the old Mayflower house for his report.

"The idea was fair game," he told Ralph. "But it sure left me without another idea, until Tennis came to my rescue!"

"Want to check out Riverland now?" Tennis asked. "It's still plenty light out."

Quacky agreed it was a great idea, since he could also keep an eye out for Puddles as they rode their bikes into the south part of town, where he had not yet had a chance to look.

"Let me know if you need any help at the Mayflower house," Quacky called out to Ralph as he and Tennis began biking away. "I've been inside there now, and it isn't spooky. At least I don't think *it's* haunted!"

As they pedaled, Quacky asked Tennis to tell him what he meant by saying he thought Riverland was haunted.

"Well, I've only been there twice, actually," Tennis admitted. "And not for long, either time. I just sort of rode my bike into that part of town one day, trying to learn more about Smedley and what's here. When I went inside Riverland, I thought it looked kind of neat, like an old movie set in Hollywood that had been abandoned for years. Then I went inside Aladdin's Castle, the old spook-house at Riverland, and I got the strange feeling that it's haunted or something."

"Aladdin's Castle?" Quacky had never been there.

"It's a big building in the shape of a head," Tennis explained. "It's the head of Aladdin, from the fairy tale about the Wonderful Lamp, you know? He has a long, black mustache and wears a turban. It's really only a big, wooden front for a building about three stories high, and it has some basements under it. It's full of spooky rooms."

"How come you think it's haunted?"

"Well, first of all, when I went in there last week, I had a sandwich with me. Ham and cheese on rye," Tennis explained further. "I set it down for a minute, to explore around the castle, and when I came back for it, it was gone."

"Maybe rats," Quacky figured. "Gosh, it's not going to be much fun checking out Aladdin's Castle if it's full of rats."

"I don't think it was rats that took the sandwich. I didn't see any around. But while I was walking around inside the castle, I got the uneasy feeling something or somebody was *watching* me. You know how sometimes you can sort of tell that somebody is staring at you, even if your eyes are closed or your back is turned to them?"

Quacky knew the feeling. He had awakened many a morning when he sensed Puddles staring at him beside his bed. It was Puddles's way of telling Quacky he was either hungry or had to go out and do his things.

"Well, if it wasn't rats, and I hope it wasn't," Quacky told him, "I'm sure it wasn't ghosts. I believe in a lot of things, but not ghosts."

Tennis didn't look as certain as Quacky that ghosts did not exist.

"Well, somebody took my sandwich and was keeping a close eye on me that day," Tennis insisted.

"What about the second time you went there?" Quacky asked as they kept pedaling, all the while keeping an eye out for Puddles.

"The second time was just three days ago," Tennis reported. "I was just coming out of what used to be the old barrel ride in Aladdin's Castle. It's a big room the shape of a huge barrel, all out of wood. Back when the castle and Riverland were packed with people having fun, I guess the barrel spun around. So you tried to crawl through on your hands and knees, but meantime the floor and walls and roof kept turning in a circle."

"Sounds like fun!" Quacky said.

"Yeah, but it wasn't fun for me, because while I was in the barrel, and it wasn't moving, I thought I heard voices!"

"*Human* voices?" Quacky wasn't even sure why he asked that.

"I guess they were human. I've never heard a ghost or a vampire or a werewolf talk, have you? Anyway, they were voices, like men talking. Only I couldn't hear what they were saying. And then, as if they knew I overheard them, they clammed up, and I didn't hear them anymore."

"Weird," Quacky agreed. "But I still don't think ghosts are haunting the place."

"You may change your mind when we get there," Tennis told him.

When they reached the high wooden fence and gate of Riverland, Quacky saw that the place was a lot bigger than he had expected.

He had never been inside Riverland before, since it had been closed down long before he and Aunt Maggie came to Smedley.

Signs posted all over the fence said "CLOSED!" "KEEP OUT!" "DO NOT TRESPASS!" But Quacky knew no signs were going to keep him out of any place!

Tennis showed Quacky some broken slats in the fence where he had gotten inside before. They walked their bikes through and soon were in an eerie wonderland.

Quacky thought it was like being at a big carnival that had suddenly ended, with the lights all turned off and the merry-go-round music stopped. The high roller-coaster tracks still towered above them, but the moving cars and the people screaming from fun or fright were missing. A few colored plastic flags still flapped in the breeze, high above tall poles along the midway, but they were faded and torn.

"Quiet as a graveyard," Quacky couldn't help muttering as he looked around.

Although the sun was shining, there was an autumn chill in the air, and it was so quiet, all he could hear was the wind flapping the old flags high above them.

Now he and Tennis were the only two people in the park. Or *were* they?, he wondered. He began to get the uncomfortable feeling that they were not as alone as they seemed.

A big pavilion with a bandshell and stage made Quacky feel extra-lonely. Hundreds of benches stood in rows stretching all the way up to the stage, but no one was sitting on them.

"There it is, up ahead!" Tennis pointed out.

Looming in the distance at the far end of the long, wide midway was the strangest-looking building Quacky had ever seen, and the scariest.

Aladdin's Castle was all built behind the huge face of Aladdin, who in *The Arabian Nights* was the son of a poor widow in China and had a magic lamp and a genie who did his bidding. The face had a drooping black mustache. A gaudily painted silk scarf tightly covered its head and flowed down over its left ear. The giant-sized head appeared to be about four stories tall and a couple of houses wide.

"You enter through the open mouth," Tennis told Quacky. "I guess that's kind of spooky in itself."

They parked their bikes outside the castle and ran a chain through both front wheels and locked them together.

As they began walking up the steps toward Aladdin's mouth, Quacky again had the strange feeling that they were being watched. Tennis nudged him and Quacky looked up at the big, intense blue eyes of Aladdin. They seemed to be staring right through him, but somehow Quacky thought that wasn't it. Aladdin wasn't really watching them, but he had the feeling that something or someone inside the castle was.

There was no door on Aladdin's mouth, just a big opening through which the boys stepped into the castle. The first room they entered was small and square, with black walls and ceiling. It had no furniture in it, but before Quacky could wonder what it was for, Tennis pushed open a door at the far end, and they went into a big room that once had been all white but now was a dusty gray. Animal cages were painted on the walls, but no painted animals were inside them.

"One of them is a real cage," Tennis told Quacky, feeling along one wall until he found the right one. "Here it is! You push against one side of the cage, and . . . ."

All of a sudden they were sliding down a steep ramp, their feet flying over their heads.

"Hey, where are we falling?" Quacky called as they tumbled down and down.

Finally they landed on a floor at the bottom of the ramp and looked at each other.

"Wasn't that a surprise?" Tennis asked.

"You could have warned me."

"Nobody warned me, the first time."

Quacky figured it was only fair then, that Tennis pulled a surprise on him. He wondered how many more surprises he was in for.

When Quacky looked around, he noticed

that he and Tennis were both surrounded by lions and tigers. Their jaws were all opened wide, showing big, sharp teeth. But the animals were only painted on the walls.

"I'll bet when this thing was working, they had sounds of lions and tigers roaring, to scare people even more," Quacky suggested.

"Next comes the barrel room," Tennis warned him as they got on their feet. He pushed on the biggest lion, which was really another door.

It was just as Tennis had described it, Quacky saw. A big, round room shaped like the inside of a huge wooden barrel. Even though it wasn't moving and tumbling them off their feet, Quacky could hardly balance himself as he followed Tennis inside, holding first onto one side wall and then the other as they stumbled along.

Halfway through, Quacky pulled at Tennis's shirt and stopped him.

"Listen . . . Do you hear anything?" Quacky was sure he had heard something.

"No," Tennis replied, listening.

"I thought I heard voices."

"That's what I thought I heard the other day," Tennis said.

Quacky let go of Tennis's shirt and followed him the rest of the way through the barrel.

On the other side they found themselves in a dungeon. The walls and floor and ceiling were all of huge blocks of gray stone, and skeletons hung from chains fastened to the walls.

Quacky began to get the creeps. "How do we get out of here?" he asked, shivering.

"There's lots more, I think," Tennis told him. He sounded frightened.

"Later! Let's get back outside now!"

"The only way out I know is through here." Tennis led the way through the dungeon to a big, heavy wooden door right beside a hor-rible-looking torture device.

Quacky had seen one like it in an old Boris Karloff movie. He thought it was a medieval rack. Mad scientists or monster-makers chained their victims to the rack and pulled on their arms and legs until they gave in and did what was wanted of them.

He and Tennis hurried past the rack and through the big door, which led to a tunnel. The walls and ceiling were so close and low that they had to crawl through a long way on their hands and knees.

At last Tennis pushed against a door at the end of the tunnel. They found themselves out-side again, at ground level, behind the castle.

While he caught his breath from the long crawl and from being frightened, Quacky looked at the back of the castle and immedi-ately felt better.

"It doesn't look so scary from here," he ob-served. "Aladdin's face is just a big wooden frame stuck on the front of a big, old wooden building. It looks like the back lot of a movie set I saw on TV once."

"I guess there's lots more to Aladdin's Castle, but so far, that's all I've seen," Tennis replied. "What do you think of it?"

"Sure scared me," Quacky admitted. "I've had enough for now. How about you?"

"I have too."

They started to walk around one side of the castle, heading for the front again, when Quacky reached out an arm and stopped Tennis.

"Hey, listen."

Tennis listened, but didn't hear anything.

"More voices?" he asked.

"No," Quacky replied, sure this time that he had heard something. "I could swear I heard a dog barking, from inside the castle!"

When he got back home to Aunt Maggie's, Quacky was so excited he could hardly wait to tell her and Jerry all about the voices and barking he had heard at Riverland. But Jerry wasn't home, and Aunt Maggie was busy making tea and talking to two old men and two old women in her kitchen. He recognized them as some of her bridge-playing friends, but was surprised to see again that day the two men who had complained to the police sergeant that morning about the disco shoes.

"Quacky, I'll listen to you a little later," Aunt Maggie told him impatiently. "First, I'd like to introduce you to some old friends of mine who are going to come live with us."

He was glad the two old men didn't recognize him from the police station, because he didn't want them to know he had overheard their quarrel about the shoes. They were on the other feet now, being worn by the better-dressed man with the mustache. The man who had worn the disco shoes in the police station now wore the old brown shoes.

He didn't know the others, the two old ladies, by name, though he had seen them at the house before. Aunt Maggie was usually too busy to introduce Quacky to her house guests. He wished they had all come over later, after he'd had a chance to tell Aunt Maggie and Jerry about the voices and the barking he heard in Aladdin's Castle.

Aunt Maggie introduced the ladies first. The lady with the tiny-sounding name, Midge Cooper, was big and fat. The lady with the big-sounding name, Ella (short for elephant, Quacky figured) Grately, was short and skinny, almost as frail-looking as Mattie Mayflower.

The man with the mustache and currently wearing the disco shoes was introduced as Morton Horton. His companion went by the name of Frank Norton. No wonder they get confused about whose shoes they're wearing,

Quacky thought, since even their names were so alike. They even looked like twins, except that one had the mustache. Otherwise they were both tall and as skinny as garden rakes.

"They're going to take the rooms up in the attic," Aunt Maggie told Quacky after introducing him. "Jerry says that after the ceilings dry out, he can plaster the cracks the rain drips made. He's put some tar over the cracks already, but it won't keep us dry if we get another heavy rain."

"We won't be staying long, Quacky," Midge Cooper assured him. "Maggie is awfully generous, letting us stay here for so little rent!"

"We wouldn't accept her generosity, except we have no place else to go," Ella Grately added.

"We had to be out of our apartments by today," Morton Horton explained, admiring his disco shoes.

"Can you give me a hand with my suitcases?" Frank Norton asked Quacky.

"He's got half my clothes in them," Morton Horton grumbled under his breath, but everyone heard him.

The ladies looked embarrassed that their gentlemen friends from the apartment building were still bickering.

Well, at least Horton and Norton will finally get rooms of their own, Quacky thought, lifting one of Norton's heavy suitcases. Norton took

the other one and Horton followed them upstairs with one of his own.

"Maggie, I don't know what we'd have done
without you," Midge told Aunt Maggie when
Quacky came down to help them with their
bags.

"I guess we'd be out in the street," Ella concluded.

While the new house guests talked in the
parlor over tea, Aunt Maggie busied herself in
the kitchen, and Quacky impatiently tried to
tell her about his adventures that afternoon at
Riverland and Aladdin's Castle.

"I think I heard a dog barking, from inside
the castle," Quacky told her, finishing his story.

"Well, what about it?" she asked, handing
him a tray of lunch meats and cheese to take
out to the parlor.

"Well, I don't think it was just any dog's
bark. I think it was Puddles!"

"Oh, Quacky, don't you think you're hearing
things?" she asked. "You just miss him so, you
think you're hearing him bark. I'll bet it wasn't
even a bark. An old building like that probably
creaks, and you just thought it sounded like a
dog barking."

Quacky was sure it wasn't the building
creaking, old as it was.

"I used to go to Riverland almost every Saturday," Horton told Quacky as the meat and
cheese plate was placed in front of him. "I

couldn't help overhear you talking about it. Is Aladdin's Castle still there?"

"Spooky as ever," Quacky replied, going back to the kitchen.

Aunt Maggie gave him another plate with rye bread, and he brought that to the guests.

"I used to operate the parachute ride at Riverland," Norton said proudly, making himself a big sandwich.

"I'll never forget the first time you sneaked me a ride, for free," Ella exclaimed.

Quacky was surprised the parachute ever brought her down, she was so tiny and seemed to weigh so little.

"Oh, I remember the handsomest carnival barker there on the midway," Midge Cooper declared. "His name was Felix Morgnester, but he was much better looking than his name. When the midway closed, and they padlocked Riverland, he just sort of disappeared. All these years, I've wondered whatever became of him."

"Probably pushed on to another carnival," Norton suggested. He was the first to make himself a sandwich, and it kept getting bigger. Horton and the ladies gave him a look of reprimand, but he went on building it higher and higher with rye bread and cheese and lunch meat.

"So it's abandoned now," Midge said sadly. "I remember some mighty good times there. Es-

DEL ROBLE SCHOOL LIBRARY

pecially in the pavilion. I sang opera there once. I had hopes then of an opera career, before I turned to nursing. I never died so well as I did there at Riverland, as Marguerite in *Faust*, one Sunday in August, in 1942, I think it was."

Quacky brought a relish tray of olives and some of Aunt Maggie's homemade hot pickles to the parlor. A few minutes later, after Aunt Maggie brought a pot of hot coffee into the room, and Quacky followed with an angel-food cake, they all heard the front doorbell ring.

"Now I wonder who that can be?" Aunt Maggie asked. "Quacky, see who's there?"

"Maybe it's someone, with Puddles!" he said excitedly, running to the front door and still holding the cake.

Mattie Mayflower stood trembling on the doorstep as Quacky opened the door.

When he called to tell Aunt Maggie who was there, she hurried to see what Miss Mayflower wanted. Quacky could see that his aunt was as surprised as he was to see Mattie Mayflower calling on them. He had never known her to come over before.

"Pattie's gone again, and I don't know what to do!" the tiny old lady cried. "Look what I just found, with my mail."

She handed Aunt Maggie a note, and Quacky read it aloud over his aunt's shoulder.

"Dear Rich Lady—I got *two* dogs now, and they look like two peas in a pod, except for one thing. One's a male and the other's a female. I'm gonna give you a bargain offer . . . both dogs for $600 cash! Because they're driving me nuts, trying to escape.

"Tomorrow, Saturday, go to the South Branch of the Smedley Public Library at two o'clock. Put the $600 cash inside a copy of *The Call of the Wild* by Jack London. *AND DON'T CALL THE COPS!*

"When I get the money, you get your dogs back. At three o'clock, go to the Dog Pound, and you'll find them there."

Quacky looked from Aunt Maggie to Mattie Mayflower. "Now they've got Puddles *and* Pattie!" he cried.

5

THE CALL
OF THE WILD

"But I'm *not* rich!" Mattie Mayflower exclaimed as Aunt Maggie took her hand and drew her inside the house. She looked ready to faint, Quacky thought. "I don't have six *dollars* to spare, much less six *hundred!*"

Aunt Maggie helped Miss Mayflower to the couch and her new house guests listened sympathetically as the old woman explained further:

"Just because I live in a big, old house doesn't mean I'm rich. The family money went a long time ago, mostly to back taxes. I've had to sell almost all the antique furniture, to keep up with taxes and bills."

So she isn't stingy or hoarding her money,

Quacky realized. She really is too poor to have electricity!

Aunt Maggie had Quacky bring a hot cup of coffee for Miss Mayflower. Before she had time to take a sip, Jerry came home and joined them in the parlor while she told them more:

"I don't want to burden you with my problems, but I just don't know how I can pay six hundred dollars to get Pattie back. But I just *have* to have her back. She's . . . she's all I have."

"You poor dear," Aunt Maggie comforted her. "Now just don't you worry. If the dognappers have both Puddles and Pattie, the least we can do is split the ransom amount, fifty-fifty. But I don't know where *I* can come up with three hundred dollars myself!"

"We should call the cops," Jerry suggested. Everyone looked at him.

"But the dognappers warn not to call the police," Quacky reminded him. "They might take it out on Puddles and Pattie, if we sic the police on them."

Aunt Maggie was doing some thinking.

"It's a bad business, to pay ransom money," she told them. "It just encourages the dognappers to steal more dogs, making more people suffer."

"But I want Pattie back!" Miss Mayflower was near tears.

"Maybe there's some way for us to trap the

dognappers," Quacky suggested. Now all eyes turned on him. He had been doing a lot of thinking, ever since he read the first ransom note the night before. A plan was forming in his head.

"We could put the money in the book at the library and then catch whoever takes it off the shelf."

"We might catch the dognapper, but still not get the dogs back," Jerry warned. "I think I ought to just call Sally and let her handle this."

Jerry was referring to Lieutenant Sally O'Rourke of the Smedley Police Department. They were practically engaged, and Quacky figured that some day she would be his new mother, and Jerry his new father, if they adopted him. He could hardly wait, especially to have his friend Jerry be his father.

But Quacky didn't want Jerry to call the policewoman or anyone else at the police department. He was still afraid of what the dognappers might do to Puddles, and Pattie, if they were double-crossed.

"We could put some fake money in an envelope and put it inside the book," Quacky suggested. "Some of my pals and I could stand around by the shelf where *The Call of the Wild* is kept. We could be pretending to be looking for books, but because we'd be around, the dognapper wouldn't risk opening the envelope. He'd just take the book and check it out. We could follow him after that. He'd probably go wherever the dogs are being held. Then we could catch the dognappers and get back the dogs, and it wouldn't cost us anything."

It wasn't a bad plan, the others agreed. Even Jerry said he thought it might work. At least, he said, it was worth a try.

"We can use some Monopoly money!" Quacky suggested. "And my pals Tennis and Ralph and Will and Katie could go with me to the library tomorrow and plant it in an envelope inside the book. We can follow whoever checks it out afterward, on our bikes."

"Well, I can't be there to keep an eye on you, so be careful," Aunt Maggie said.

"I've got to work at the mortuary." Jerry added.

After the plans were made, Mattie Mayflower shyly accepted Aunt Maggie's invitation to move their afternoon tea party to the dining room.

Quacky could see that Miss Mayflower was in some kind of pain. When she got up from the couch, she sort of limped to the dining-room table.

"Are you feeling well, dear?" Aunt Maggie asked her.

"It's just my arthritis," Miss Mayflower explained, as if she didn't want to bring up any more of her problems. "Sometimes it's hard to walk."

"I was a nurse for many years," Midge Cooper explained. "You probably could do with some heat and massage. I'll walk back home with you later, if you'd like, and see if I can help you a little."

"That would be very kind of you," Miss Mayflower replied gratefully.

"Quacky can get my old hot-water bottle from the medicine cabinet upstairs," Aunt Maggie added. "And I've got a jar of some heating salve that's helped my arthritis. You can take that, too, Mattie."

"I've got a cane you can use," Morton Horton volunteered. "I'll go with you and Midge, and show you how to walk with it."

Quacky could see how pleased Aunt Maggie was that her friends were taking an interest in helping Mattie Mayflower. It was just as he had thought before. When you tune in to helping other people with problems, you start to forget your own.

It reminded him of something he had heard a long time ago, at an orphanage he had been stuck in for a while. About a man with no shoes who felt sorry for himself, until he saw a man with no feet.

That made Quacky think of Morton Horton

and Frank Norton, arguing about who was the rightful owner of the shiny black disco shoes. He figured that Mr. Horton couldn't be such a bad guy, if he was concerned enough about Miss Mayflower's arthritis to lend her his cane.

Later that evening, Quacky called Tennis, Will, and Katie and they all said they would meet him at the library before two o'clock the next day. Afterward, he went next door and told Ralph his plan, when they were alone in Ralph's room, so his father, the police chief, couldn't hear.

"Don't you think you ought to tell the police?" Ralph asked. "The big money the dog-nappers are demanding makes them pretty big-time operators. They might be dangerous."

"If you're scared, you don't have to come tomorrow," Quacky challenged.

"I'm not scared! Who said I was scared?" Ralph demanded. "I just thought you ought to bring the police in on it."

"I would, except I'm afraid Puddles might get hurt, and Pattie, too."

"I don't suppose you care all that much about what happens to Pattie."

It made Quacky think a minute. No, he had to admit, he was a lot more worried about Puddles than he was about Pattie. But wasn't that only natural?, he asked himself.

"The main thing is, we try to get them both

back safe," Quacky told Ralph. "You going to help me or not?"

"Sure, I'll help you," Ralph replied. "You'd help me, if dognappers had Clemontis Regis, wouldn't you?"

Quacky knew he didn't have to answer that.

When he got back home, Aunt Maggie told Quacky to call Ernestine MacDougall, the wife of the president of the First National Bank of Smedley.

He wondered what Mrs. MacDougall could be calling him for, and quickly rang her up on the kitchen phone.

"Quacky, I've got a big favor to ask you," she told him. Jerry and Aunt Maggie were playing chess on the kitchen table while Ella Grately and Frank Norton watched. He figured that Midge Cooper and Morton Horton had taken Miss Mayflower back to her house.

"Sure, anything," Quacky assured Mrs. Mac-Dougall. He knew he was forever in debt to Chester MacDougall, her husband, for helping Jerry get a light prison sentence for bank robbery. And then helping Jerry get a work-parole as apprentice mortician to Nick Stitch in town.

"Well, I've sprained an ankle and won't be able to take Jennifer-Louise for walks for a while," Mrs. MacDougall explained.

Quacky hadn't known the MacDougalls had little children. He thought they were childless.

"She gets so upset and nervous if she doesn't get her afternoon walk in the park," Mrs. Mac-Dougall went on. "I thought of you right away, Quacky. You like pets."

"Pets?" Quacky wondered what kind of a pet Jennifer-Louise was.

"My Angora cat, Jennifer-Louise," Mrs. Mac-Dougall explained. "I always take her for a walk in the afternoon, in Centennial Park, on a leash. Can you do that for me, tomorrow and for the next few days, until my ankle is better? I'll pay you three dollars for an hour."

It was about the last thing Quacky wanted to be bothered with the next afternoon, but he gave in. "Sure, Mrs. MacDougall, I'll walk your cat." He almost laughed at the thought of himself walking a cat on a leash. "What time tomorrow?"

"Jennifer-Louise is so fussy about keeping appointments and being on a regular routine. I always walk her from two to three o'clock. Will that fit into your day tomorrow?"

It couldn't fit in worse!, Quacky groaned. How can I handle walking a cat on a leash when at the same time I'm supposed to be staking out the library for the dognapper and following him to find Puddles and Pattie?

His first instinct was to say he was sorry, that he had forgotten something and just couldn't walk her cat from two to three o'clock. But then he remembered again how much he and Jerry owed Mister McDougall for all his help.

"That'll be okay, Mrs. MacDougall," he assured her. "I'll come by for Jennifer at a quarter to two, if it's okay."

"That'll be fine, Quacky," Mrs. MacDougall agreed. "But *do* call her by her full name, Jennifer-*Louise*. She feels awfully slighted if she's just called Jennifer. They were my mother's and sister's names, so naturally I gave them both to her."

Naturally, Quacky thought.

He didn't expect Aunt Maggie and Jerry and the others to keep a straight face when he told them why Mrs. MacDougall had called.

That night, before he went to bed, Quacky took his Monopoly game out of his closet and sorted out the play money. He selected twelve fifty-dollar denominations, stuffed them in a small white envelope, sealed it, and rested it against a photo of himself and Puddles that stood on his dresser top.

"Be seeing you tomorrow, Puddles," he assured his dog and himself. But then he found he couldn't fall asleep, for wondering how he was going to walk a cat and catch a dognapper, all at the same time!

6

A MAN'S BARK

A particularly loud rumble of thunder followed by about the sharpest crack of lightning he ever heard awakened Quacky early Saturday morning. Through blurry eyes he looked at his clock on the dresser and saw that it was only half past five.

Seconds later, he heard the rain pounding. It began raining cats and dogs. He had to laugh, thinking how appropriate it was, since today he was going to be mixed up with both animals.

"Jerry! It's raining inside the house again!" he heard Aunt Maggie call out in the hall.

Soon he heard the old people upstairs in the attic, stomping around. The roof!, he figured. It's leaking again.

Quacky ran out of his room in his boxer shorts and collided with Jerry, who had left his bedroom in such a hurry that he hadn't put on a robe. He was clad only in a pair of fire-engine red silk pajamas that Quacky remembered from Uncle Otis's collection.

Aunt Maggie, rushing from her room, crashed into them both, then wrapped her robe around herself, and led the way upstairs. They found the new house guests all trying to dodge water leaking through the ceiling cracks.

Another bucket brigade went into action, this time with more brigadiers than buckets. After Aunt Maggie had every pot, pan, pail, bucket, bowl, and flower vase in the house positioned under a fast drip, she gave up.

"The rest we'll just have to get with a mop," she wailed, looking helplessly at Jerry, whose pajamas were soaking wet.

"Soon as the roof dries, I'll put up new shingles," he promised.

"I'll get you another pair of Otis's pajamas," she replied. "But I don't know where I'll get the money to fix the roof."

"Maybe you can take out a second mortgage on the house," Jerry suggested, wringing water out of the bottom of his pajama jacket.

"I already have one," Aunt Maggie admitted. "I told Otis he just had to get a job. Maybe that's why he left. He knew I don't get much money for writing my astrology column for the newspaper."

"We aren't paying you much rent. We could all pitch in and help you pay for a new roof," Ella Grately suggested.

Quacky thought that was very generous of the old folks.

"That is, if we had any extra money," Midge Cooper added, finishing the other lady's sentence for her.

"Maybe I can get another job. That would bring in more money," Jerry suggested. "I could still work at the mortuary and keep my Fix-It Shop."

"Two jobs are too many, I wouldn't think of you working three!" Aunt Maggie said, looking sympathetically at Jerry. "Why, if it wasn't for you, we wouldn't even have *this* roof over our heads."

Quacky knew Jerry was doing all he could to bring in money and fix up the old house.

"It's not your problem, any of you, it's mine," Aunt Maggie told them. "But I appreciate your wanting to help, anyway. I guess we can all go back to bed, now that most of the drips are covered. I don't suppose I'll be able to sleep, though."

She gave Jerry a big towel to dry himself and another pair of Uncle Otis's fancy silk pajamas. Quacky laughed when he saw Jerry in them, a few minutes later in Jerry's room. They were deep green, with colored butterflies all over them.

"Maybe *this* is why your Uncle Otis ran away!" Jerry quipped, modeling the loud pajamas.

Quacky and Jerry talked together, trying to figure out a way for Aunt Maggie to afford a new roof, and going over the plan to catch the dognappers. They didn't solve the first problem, and Jerry seemed especially worried about the second.

Quacky tossed in his bed afterward, unable to fall asleep again. The rain kept reminding him of cats and dogs and the busy afternoon he had ahead of him.

When he heard the rain stop later and looked again at his clock, he saw that it was a quarter to seven. He got up, washed in a hurry, dressed, and left the house even before Aunt Maggie got up to make breakfast.

Riding his bike away from the house, Quacky wished he had taken a jacket along. It was late October and cold. Lots of leaves that had been rusty or golden on the maple and elm trees just the day before the rainstorm now lay flat and wet on the sidewalks and streets.

Tomorrow it'll be Halloween, Quacky realized. I sure hope I find Puddles before then! It'll be our first Halloween together, and I don't want him to be afraid.

On the off chance that Puddles had escaped from his captors, Quacky wanted to make another search for him. He pedaled up one block and down the next, then crossed between blocks, to make sure he covered them completely, looking under every porch and behind every bush he could. Still he saw no sign of Puddles.

Before long, he found himself in front of Tennis Harper's house, a few blocks from Aunt Maggie's. Tennis was out back in the yard, emptying the garbage.

"Thought maybe we'd check out Riverland this morning," Quacky suggested.

"I can't," Tennis said, disappointed. "My folks are playing indoor tennis at a tournament this morning at the country club. I've got to sit with my baby sister, Backhand."

"Backhand! They named your little sister *Backhand?*"

"It's not her real name," Tennis explained. "Just her nickname. Her real name is Alice, like in Wonderland. But she gave Dad a black eye once, with the back of her hand, swinging it out of her crib. He figures she's gonna become a big tennis pro, when she grows up, with a backhand like that."

"For sure!" Quacky said, laughing and starting to ride off. "I'll probably go to Riverland anyway, myself, and look around. Maybe I can find out if that was Puddles I heard barking there yesterday. See you at the South Branch of the library around two o'clock?"

"I'll be there, with the others," Tennis assured him. "Good luck!"

Quacky waved and rode away toward Riverland on the south side of town. Pedaling hard, the cool morning breeze made him feel colder. The colder he felt, the more he thought of Halloween, coming just the next day, Sunday. And the more he thought of Halloween, the more he thought of spooky things like skeletons and ghosts. He knew he was putting himself in a great scary state of mind to be checking out Aladdin's Castle all by himself.

A short time later, locking his bike outside the castle, Quacky felt Aladdin's eyes staring at him again. But he faced the giant head and walked up the stairs and into the castle again, through the mouth.

When he entered the small square room with the black walls and ceiling, he still felt as if eyes were on him, as Tennis had, but, he figured, they couldn't be Aladdin's. Aladdin's eyes were trained straight ahead, outside. Someone or something was looking at him *inside*, he was sure.

He pushed the door open at the far end of the room and entered the big gray room with cages painted on the walls. He was not very anxious to pass through the room and push on the real cage that would take him tumbling down the steep ramp.

Just then he felt someone grab him by an arm. He was being pulled back!

He was about to cry out for help when a hand covered his mouth. He struggled to get free from whoever was holding him, but he couldn't. And he couldn't turn his head and see who it was, either.

After a bit, the hand left Quacky's mouth, and he was turned around, to face an old man.

"Don't worry, Sonny, I won't hurt you."

He wasn't very tall, Quacky observed quickly. His hair was gray and long and needed cutting even more than Quacky's own hair. He wore old clothes and looked kind of down and out.

"I didn't want you making any noise, to maybe bring the police here," the man explained. "They don't know I live here."

"You live here!" Quacky exclaimed.

"Oh, you think I'm a ghost or something?" the old man asked. The idea was written all over Quacky's frightened face.

"Well, I don't really believe in ghosts," Quacky hedged, trying to look brave. He wasn't all that sure about ghosts anymore.

"I used to work here at Riverland, a long time ago. I was a carny barker, on the midway." The old man looked proud of what he had once been.

"Then you're . . . ." Quacky remembered who Midge Cooper had told him about, just the day before. "You're Felix Morgensomething!"

"Morgnester," the man said, holding out a hand for Quacky to shake. "But how did you know my name?"

"That's a long story," Quacky said, shaking hands. "I never shook hands before with a gho ... with a carnival barker. You sure scared me, for a minute. But you just live here?"

"I had nowhere else to go, when Riverland closed after the war. I did leave it, and Smedley, too. I wandered around the country for years. Only found odd jobs. Since most of the carnivals closed after television came in, nobody needed the only thing I do best, bark at carnivals."

Quacky felt sorry for the old man and lost his fear of him. The man didn't ask again how he knew his name, and Quacky forgot to tell him about it.

"Then the voices my pal and I heard," Quacky wondered, looking at the man. "They were you, talking to somebody else who lives here?"

"Just me, talking to myself, I suppose," Felix explained.

"Did you take a boy's sandwich a few days ago, when he came here looking around?"

Felix looked puzzled. "No, I never saw any sandwich. Maybe a mouse took it. There's a pretty good-sized family of mice living in the castle."

"But you have a dog, I suppose." Quacky hoped against hope that the barker did *not* have a dog, so that the barking he heard the day before might still have been Puddles, calling to him.

"Yes, I've a little schnauzer named Peppi. I always used a dog in my act, but not always a schnauzer. Peppi got away from me in the castle, and I was looking for him when I came upon you. I try to discourage kids from hanging around the castle. Not because they might discover me and tell the police I'm living here, but because they might get hurt. It's an old, dilapidated building, and lots of boards come loose and might hurt you."

He looked at Quacky as if asking him not to give him away.

"Don't worry," Quacky assured him. "I won't tell the police you're here. But how do you *live*, in such an old place?"

"Not easy, but at least I don't have to pay any rent. I go out at night for any food I can beg. I guess that's really what I've become, after all those years of being a barker . . . a beggar."

"Hey, I'm gonna earn three dollars this afternoon, and I've got almost a dollar in change on me right now." Quacky dug into a pocket of his jeans and took out some nickels and dimes and a quarter and some pennies.

He could see the man didn't want to take his contribution, but was too broke to refuse it.

"I can come back later today with the three dollars," Quacky promised. "I've got to walk a lady's cat."

The old man laughed and then confessed that he hadn't laughed that hard in years.

"My pal Tennis and I thought the castle was haunted!" Quacky admitted to the old man. "Now I can tell him it's only been you, and your schnauzer!"

The old man looked at him kind of funny, Quacky thought.

"Oh, but I think you may still be right about that haunting business," Felix replied. He looked over Quacky's head and gazed at the walls where the lion and tiger cages were painted.

You're just saying that, to scare me away, Quacky thought.

"No, I ain't," Felix assured him.

"No, you ain't what?" Quacky asked, studying him.

"Just saying that to scare you away from here."

Now Quacky *was* scared.

"How'd you know what I was thinking?" he asked.

"I guess all those years I worked on the midway, I learned some of the tricks of the trade. I used to go out with a lady mind reader."

"But you don't have to scare me away," Quacky told him. "I won't tell anybody you live here, and I'll be careful of loose boards. But do you really think the place is haunted?"

"All I know is, *I* hear noises sometimes. Voices, mostly. But I've never seen anybody else here. Except twice now, I've seen a tall, thin boy with short blond hair. He's been snooping around."

"That's my pal, Tennis Harper, the one I told you about." Quacky explained how Tennis got his name, because his folks were tennis freaks. He thought they could both use another laugh about then, so he told Felix about Backhand. The old man laughed harder than before.

Quacky then explained why he and Tennis had come there the day before, to check out the place for their Social Studies class.

"You said you saw my pal here twice," Quacky asked. "What about yesterday, when he and I were both around here. Didn't you see him and me, snooping around?"

"Yesterday?" the old man questioned, thinking hard about something. "Yesterday I wasn't here. I was out along the river, fishing. I didn't get back until just a little while ago."

He wasn't going to tell Felix everything he knew. Quacky decided that he would keep yesterday's events to himself, now that he knew the voices and maybe even the barking he had heard the day before had *not* come from Felix or his schnauzer after all. Maybe there *are* ghosts in Aladdin's Castle at that!, he thought. And maybe the dog I heard barking *was* Puddles!

"You'd better be going now, don't you think?" old Felix Morgnester told Quacky. He got the feeling the old man was telling him, more than asking.

"Yeah, I guess you're right," Quacky agreed, though he still wanted to check out the castle more.

"Don't forget to come back with the three dollars," Felix called after him as Quacky began going back out the way he had come. "And don't tell the police!"

Don't tell the police! Quacky had heard, or read, that several times lately. It was in both ransom notes!, he remembered.

Oh, no! It couldn't be . . . Felix couldn't be the dognapper! Or *could* he?

Could the castle still be haunted?, he also wondered. And could Puddles be there, somewhere?

He wanted to go back, but when he looked behind him he saw the old carny barker waving to him from the doorway-mouth of Aladdin's Castle. He's making sure he sees me ride my bike away, Quacky decided.

Well, for now, I'll just have to do what he wants. But maybe when I come back later this afternoon, with the three dollars from walking Mrs. MacDougall's cat, I can find out more about him and his ghosts and maybe find Puddles, too!

7

QUACKY TO THE RESCUE!

Quacky rode away from Riverland, but then doubled back and re-entered the abandoned amusement park from the rear. He hoped to look around without Felix Morgnester seeing him, and maybe to hear the bark of the dog he thought might be Puddles.

But it was quiet in the park, and he heard no barking or voices, so he rode away again. He figured Jerry would be working at Nick Stitch's Funeral Parlor by then, so he biked over. He was anxious to tell him about everything.

Jerry was unloading some floral wreaths from a delivery truck out in back of the mortuary. Quacky figured it would be okay to tell

Jerry about Felix living at Aladdin's Castle, because all Felix had asked was that Quacky not
tell the police.

"I don't think that's a very good place for
you to hang around, Quacky," Jerry cautioned
him after hearing it all. "This guy Felix doesn't
sound that great to me, hiding out in a closed
amusement park. Are you sure he's all there? It
sounds to me like he might not be playing with
a full deck."

Quacky caught it and laughed. He had never
before heard that said of anyone who might be
a little crazy.

"I think he's all right. Maybe just a little
strange, from living all alone in a spook-house
for so long."

"Just the same, I think it'd be a good idea if
you didn't go there anymore," Jerry insisted.

Quacky helped Jerry carry the last of the
flowers inside the chapel. Quacky knew Jerry
had more work to do that morning. Just then
he heard Ralph call to him, from outside.

"I've been looking all over for you," Ralph
said when Quacky went out. "I thought you
might do me a favor this morning."

Quacky told Jerry he'd see him later. He was
glad to get away without having to promise
that he'd never go back to Riverland.

"I thought maybe you'd go with me to learn
more about Mattie Mayflower's house for the

Social Studies assignment," Ralph explained.

Quacky said he had time that morning and would like to be in on Ralph's investigation. Down deep, he knew why Ralph wanted him along. Ralph was too scared to check out Miss Mayflower's place himself, and Quacky didn't really blame him.

They rode their bikes to the Mayflower house. As Quacky led the way up the walk to the front door, Ralph looked all around him anxiously. "I bet bats hang out around this place," he told Quacky. "Up there on the roof."

"It's not so bad, once you've been here a couple of times," Quacky assured him. Still, Quacky felt uneasy himself. The sun was behind some dark clouds; it was getting windy again, and leaves were blowing around them. It was the first time he had come to Miss Mayflower's front door without Jerry. He half expected someone to put a hand on his shoulder and stop him, as Felix had done back at Aladdin's Castle.

"This sure would be a spooky place to come tomorrow night, on Halloween," Ralph said. He stayed so close behind Quacky that when Quacky stopped at the front door, Ralph bumped into him.

Quacky remembered that the house had no electricity, so the doorbell would not ring.

When Miss Mayflower had not answered his

knocking after a few minutes, Quacky knocked harder. Still there was no answer.

"She never goes out in the daytime," Quacky worried. "Maybe she's deaf, or very hard of hearing."

When his louder knocking still did not bring Miss Mayflower to the door, Quacky tried the doorknob.

"It's open!" he exclaimed with surprise.

"Maybe we should come back later," Ralph suggested. Quacky could see his friend was scared, even more than he was himself.

"Let's just take a little look inside," Quacky said, opening the door wide enough so he could enter the house.

Ralph followed so closely behind him, Quacky could feel his friend's breath on his neck.

"Sure is dark and quiet inside." Quacky stood and peered from the entrance hall into the parlor and through to the dining room and kitchen. He didn't see any lights on in any of the rooms.

"Let's come back later," Ralph half pleaded.

"There's nothing to be afraid of," Quacky insisted. He was gaining more confidence. "The place isn't haunted. She's just a poor old lady living alone in a big old house."

Most of the big, high windows were covered with heavy drapes, and sunlight, even when there was any, could not brighten the rooms. Quacky thought it looked like midnight in the house, even though it was still not noon.

"What was *that?*" Ralph grabbed Quacky by an arm.

Ralph's cry was so loud it startled Quacky.

"What was what?"

"A sort of moaning," Ralph explained.

"I didn't hear anything," Quacky told him.

They stopped at the doorway to the parlor. The room was dark, but they could see white sheets covering a big couch and two stuffed chairs. Otherwise the room was completely empty.

A soft, eerie moaning reached their ears, sounding as if it were coming from above somewhere.

"Now *I* hear it!" Quacky exclaimed.

They shushed each other and listened intently. They looked up, half expecting to find an owl or a ghost floating along the parlor ceiling, wailing down to them. But all they saw was a cut-glass chandelier with cobwebs hanging from the big, empty ceiling.

"I think it's coming from upstairs," Quacky judged.

"Well, then for sure, let's come back later!" Ralph began to pull Quacky away, but Quacky resisted.

"You can go, if you want. *I'm* going upstairs to see where the moaning's coming from."

"Maybe it's a ghost, or somebody's dead upstairs." Ralph looked as if he wanted no part of either solution.

His second suggestion was what worried Quacky. He began walking slowly toward the winding staircase between the parlor and dining room that led upstairs.

"You coming with me?" Quacky asked.

Ralph looked undecided as to whether he should try leaving the house alone or sticking with Quacky. Finally he chose to follow Quacky.

They climbed up the creaky stairs slowly, listening with each step, but they did not hear any more groans. When they reached the second floor and stood in the long, narrow hallway, they had to choose which room to look in first. Half a dozen doors led off the hall into what Quacky supposed were bedrooms. All the doors were closed except one.

Quacky inched his way toward the half-opened door at the far end of the hall. Ralph held fearfully onto Quacky's arm and followed close behind.

"Are you *sure* this place isn't haunted?" Ralph asked.

"Of *course* I'm not sure!" Quacky told him, and saw that the effect he wanted to make on Ralph had succeeded. Ralph looked pale as a ghost.

"There it is again!" Ralph cried out. First he

let go of Quacky's arm and started to run for the stairs. Then he ran back and grabbed Quacky for protection as Quacky kept walking toward the room with the half-opened door.

When they reached the far room, Quacky slowly pushed the door open and peeked inside.

Miss Mayflower was lying on the floor in her nightgown, beside her big four-poster bed. Her eyes were closed. She was moaning and seemed to be in pain.

Quacky ran to her as Ralph stood trembling in the doorway.

"Don't move me, Quacky, but I'm very glad you came," Miss Mayflower told him weakly, trying to raise her head off the floor. "I thought no one would come and find me for days, after it was all over."

After she died, Quacky thought, kneeling over the old lady and feeling sorry for her. Now he was really glad he hadn't let Ralph or the moaning scare him off.

"I hurt my leg, when I fell beside my bed this morning," Miss Mayflower explained. "I guess I need a doctor. But don't try to lift me up. Something might happen, if you move me. But would you put a pillow under my head, please?"

Quacky got a pillow and wrapped a blanket around her before he started for the door.

"I'll go right home and phone for a doctor to

come help you," Quacky told her. "Ralph will stay here with you."

"*I'll* go phone for a doctor!" Ralph said, anxious to get out of there.

Quacky didn't care which one went. He wasn't afraid of Miss Mayflower or her house now.

He had a lot he wanted to ask her, about the house and herself, so he let Ralph go call for a doctor. But after Ralph left, Quacky could see that the old lady was too weak and in too much pain to talk much. She reached out a hand and patted the floor beside her.

Quacky got the message and squatted on the floor beside Miss Mayflower, so she wouldn't have to strain her neck looking up at him. She reached out weakly for his hand and held it.

"I'm so glad you came, Quacky." Her voice was so soft, he could hardly hear her. "I don't know what would have become of me if you hadn't. I guess I don't know how to use that cane very well. When I leaned on it, getting out of bed, it gave way, and I fell."

She didn't say much more, and after a while Aunt Maggie came. Quacky wasn't surprised to see that Ralph wasn't with her. He supposed Ralph had had enough of the spooky old house.

Well, that's okay, he thought. He would talk to Miss Mayflower himself, when she was feeling better, and learn more about the old house.

"Doctor Ruggles is on his way here," Aunt Maggie soothed Miss Mayflower, going to her side to comfort her. "He's young, but very nice. He'll be here in just a few minutes."

Miss Mayflower closed her eyes and fell into a light doze.

Quacky explained softly to his aunt how Miss Mayflower had fallen and hurt herself.

"Good thing you looked in on her this morning," Aunt Maggie told him. "Ralph told me why you both came. That'll have to wait a while now, until she's feeling better."

After a while, Quacky heard a knock at the front door and ran downstairs to let the doctor in.

Tom Ruggles, a nice-looking young doctor with straight blond hair and big, round, black-rimmed glasses, was wearing a raincoat over a sportcoat and slacks. Carrying a black medical case, he followed Quacky upstairs.

Quacky waited outside the bedroom with Aunt Maggie as the doctor inspected Miss Mayflower. After a short time, Dr. Ruggles called them back in.

"She doesn't seem to have any broken bones," he explained. "I think she just twisted herself, falling, and is sore from that. I'd like to get her to the hospital, to have some X rays taken, but she says she won't go, and she has no insurance or money to pay for X rays or hospital care. She'd rather stay home, so I'll

take care of her here. If she needs X rays later,
I'll see she gets them, and find a way for public
aid to pay her bill."

The doctor asked for Quacky's help in lifting
Miss Mayflower up onto her bed, now that he
was sure she could be moved.

"I don't want any charity!" Miss Mayflower
cried, coughing, as Dr. Ruggles and Quacky
lifted her onto her bed and covered her. "I've
never taken any public aid before, and I won't
start now!"

Dr. Ruggles smiled at Aunt Maggie and
Quacky. They could see how proud the old
woman was and sympathized with her.

"We can go into that later," Dr. Ruggles told
Miss Mayflower. "The important thing is, you
get some rest. Then you'll be like new again."

"Like new again," Mattie Mayflower said in
a faraway voice as they watched her lying
helplessly in her bed.

"She's going to need someone to look after
her for a while," Dr. Ruggles told Aunt Maggie.
"I'll have to come back to make some tests. I'll
leave some medication for her now."

"We had a retired nurse staying at our
house," Aunt Maggie told the doctor. "But she
left this morning."

Quacky looked questioningly at his aunt.

"All four of our attic guests left with their
things, before I got up this morning," Aunt
Maggie explained to him. "They left a note

saying they didn't want to be a burden to me, and they had found another place to live."

Quacky thought it was too bad. Not only had Aunt Maggie enjoyed their company, Midge Cooper could have been a big help to Miss Mayflower.

"Well then, I'll play nurse instead," Aunt Maggie assured Mattie Mayflower. "And Quacky can fill in for me, at times."

"Sure," Quacky told the old lady. "Do you play Monopoly?"

Mattie's eyes told him and the others how relieved she was that both Aunt Maggie and Quacky would be there to help her.

"The important thing is that she stay off her feet a while," Dr. Ruggles cautioned Aunt Maggie before leaving. "Now don't you worry, Miss Mayflower," he called to her from the doorway. "You'll be around and about in no time, with these people taking such good care of you."

"I just wish Pattie were here," the old lady said.

Quacky and Aunt Maggie stared at each other, wondering how they could be of help in that matter.

"Maybe by three o'clock today, Pattie *will* be back home," Quacky told Miss Mayflower, before leaving her with Aunt Maggie.

8

GOING FOR THE BAIT

There was another reason Quacky was sorry to learn that the four new house guests had left in such a hurry. He had been hoping to learn more about Riverland from them. They had all remembered the amusement park from its exciting old days, he knew.

Well, he thought, as he fixed a hot dog for his lunch, he would just have to get it all now from Felix Morgnester. He had just better not tell Jerry about going back there.

He hated to keep a secret from Jerry, or to disobey him, but he also needed to get his Social Studies information the only way he knew how, firsthand. And that meant getting it from the horse's—or rather Felix's—mouth. He figured he could find some old newspaper articles about Riverland in the library or at the newspaper office. But he also wanted to talk to people who had known it in the old days, and that didn't include Aunt Maggie because she had not moved to Smedley until after Riverland closed down.

Maybe Mattie Mayflower had gone to Riverland!, Quacky thought. He would ask her about it, as soon as she felt better.

Quacky studied the clock set into a red plastic frying pan, on the wall in Aunt Maggie's kitchen, and wolfed down some potato chips with the hot dog. Aunt Maggie was still with Mattie Mayflower and Jerry was at the mortuary. It was one-thirty, and he had to bike over to Mrs. MacDougall's to pick up Jennifer-Louise.

He pedaled hard for the MacDougall house on the near south side of Smedley. Quacky could pick up the cat and put her in his wicker bike basket and still get to the South Branch of the Smedley Library by two o'clock. He would meet his pals there in the stacks, follow the dognapper, and catch him with Puddles and Pattie and the other dogs he had stolen. Later he could walk Jennifer-Louise a little and have her back home no worse for wear.

The MacDougalls lived in the penthouse of Smedley's only high-rise apartment building, which had gone condo several years earlier.

Quacky parked his bike on the sidewalk outside and rode an elevator up to the twelfth floor. When the doors parted he found himself in the MacDougalls' hallway.

It was almost a quarter to two, according to a clock standing on a telephone table in the hall. Quacky was surprised to find Mrs. MacDougall still in a housecoat. It was a fancy, frilly pink robe, and her hair was up in curlers. He noticed that her right ankle had a bandage around it.

"Now you *will* take good care of little Jennifer-Louise, won't you, Quacky?" She cooed at the kitten she was holding.

Looking at the small white bundle of fluff, Quacky assured the bank president's wife that he would.

Mrs. MacDougall kissed the kitten on its pink nose before handing Quacky her Angora treasure. A thin, red-silk ribbon was tied around its neck. It extended into a red-ribbon leash. Quacky started sneezing, six times, one sneeze after the other in rapid succession like machine-gun fire.

"I'm allergic to cats," he explained, putting the kitten on the floor and taking her leash.

He felt funny, walking the cat by a leash into the elevator.

Before the elevator doors closed, Quacky saw Mrs. MacDougall look apprehensively at him and the cat. He thought she looked the same way Aunt Maggie had looked at him the morning when he was five years old and went off on his own to school for the first time.

When he got back downstairs, Quacky walked the kitten over to his bicycle and put her into the basket. As she squirmed and cried, trying to get out, he sneezed another six times.

"You just cooperate a little, Jennifer-Louise," he pleaded with her, "and I'll walk your little bottom off, later!"

Choked up, sneezing, and his eyes burning and watery, Quacky pedaled as hard as he could, farther south. After about ten minutes, he reached the South Branch of the Smedley Public Library. His friends were outside with their bikes. Ralph, Tennis, Will, and Katie all waved to him as he rode up.

"Who's the white panther?" Katie asked, checking out his basket.

Jennifer-Louise was squirming again and trying to claw Quacky as he sneezed six more times and explained about her.

"She won't get in the way," he assured them. "I'll tie her to a parking meter, so she doesn't wander off while we're inside."

After he accomplished that, the group went inside the library. Quacky said he knew where to find a copy of *The Call of the Wild*. They followed him along the shelves where the fiction books were kept alphabetically according to the last name of the author.

They passed the "K's" and soon were looking among the "L's" for Jack London.

"Lane, Lang, Lawrence, Leary, Levinson, Livingstone, here it is!" Quacky exclaimed. "London . . . *The Call of the Wild!*"

He took a white envelope out of his back pocket and stuck it inside the book. After returning it quickly to the shelf, he and his friends hurried into another aisle. There they waited and watched through the gaps in the stacks of books, to see who would come up to the "L's" and check out the book.

Fifteen anxious minutes passed, and the friends were growing impatient and worried. Quacky wondered whether his plan was going to work. Maybe the dognapper suspected a trap.

Then a boy of about twelve, in Levi's and a tan, zippered jacket, began scanning the books on the "K" shelves. His big glasses kept sliding down his tiny nose. He moved on to the "L's," gazing closely at the shelf, and Quacky and his friends held their breath.

Quacky was sure the boy was looking for a specific title. Quacky had pulled *The Call of the Wild* out a little from its place on the shelf, so he could keep a closer eye on it.

"He's taking it!" Quacky whispered excitedly to his friends.

He couldn't understand it! Why would a boy of twelve be a dognapper?, he wondered.

"Maybe he *isn't* the dognapper," Quacky said, as quietly as he could. "Maybe he just wants to take out the book and read it."

They watched from the stacks with open mouths as the boy took *The Call of the Wild* off the shelf and, without even opening it, carried it to the check-out woman.

"You'll enjoy this one a lot, Freddie," the librarian told the boy, taking his library card and processing it with the book. "I don't see you downstairs much. You usually take books out from upstairs, in the children's section. I'm glad to see you trying some older books."

The boy exchanged some words with her, took the book, and left.

"Let's go!" Quacky said, leading the way out of the stacks. "Maybe his father's the dognapper and he's the 'bag man', picking up the ransom money!"

Just as they were about to pass the check-out counter, Quacky looked out the front window as the boy got on his own bike.

"Oh, no!" he exclaimed. "Jennifer-Louise is gone!"

He ran out of the library, got on his bike, and began pedaling after the boy named Freddie who had taken the book with the fake ransom money inside. His pals followed close behind on their bikes.

Freddie was pedaling leisurely away, farther

south, and behind him Quacky waved to his friends, telling them not to pedal too fast. He didn't want the boy to know they were all following him.

They rode behind Freddie as he pedaled for a few blocks and then rode up a walk in the front yard of a modest, white-frame house. Quacky and his friends hid behind some cars parked on the street and watched as the boy got off his bike, leaned it against the house, and went inside.

"He's a 'front man' for the dognapper, I'll bet!" Quacky told his friends.

They left their bikes by the cars and sneaked into the yard. On tiptoes they looked inside the house through several windows.

The boy plopped down in a beanbag chair in a family room next to the kitchen and opened the book. From the boy's look of surprise when he found the envelope inside, Quacky realized his mistake. When the boy opened the envelope and stared with wonder at the Monopoly money inside, he *knew* he had been wrong.

"The wrong fish took the bait!" he wailed. "He isn't the dognapper or his 'front man.' He just wants to read the book!"

"Then how are we going to find Puddles?" Tennis asked him.

"And who took the cat?" Katie asked.

Quacky looked at them as if to say that if he

knew the answers to those questions, he would
be able to fly without an airplane.

Shortly after, facing the music at the Mac-
Dougalls' penthouse, Quacky stood expecting
the worst. Mrs. MacDougall practically fainted
upon hearing the news that Jennifer-Louise had
been *cat*napped!

"It isn't your fault, Quacky," Chester Mac-
Dougall, the bank president, told him. "It could
have happened at any time, with these dognappers on the prowl. They must have seen my
wife walking her cat in the park and were just
waiting for a chance to take Jennifer-Louise."

He didn't seem all that upset that the cat was
stolen, Quacky thought. But he could hear Mrs.
MacDougall sobbing in her bedroom. For her,
it was probably like having a child kidnapped.

"I'll offer a reward," Mr. MacDougall said,
going to the telephone. "And I'll call the police."

Quacky suggested he call the desk sergeant
and talk to one of the officers handling the dog-
napping investigation. But Mr. MacDougall told
Quacky he was used to going right to the top
when he did any kind of business.

"Chief Dooley?" Mr. MacDougall asked into
the phone, looking at Quacky as they stood in
the fancy parlor of the condominium. "Chester
here. Say, my wife's cat was just stolen. We
think it's the work of that dognapper who's

been so busy in town lately. I guess he's branching out into cats now. You'll get right on it, won't you? By the way, when are you having your next Policeman's Ball?"

Quacky could not hear what Police Chief Dooley, the father of his friend Ralph, replied to the bank president. But he knew what point Mr. MacDougall was making. The bank president would buy some tickets to the Policeman's Ball if Chief Dooley got Mrs. MacDougall's cat back.

Now *that's* a lesson in Social Studies, Quacky thought.

9

MATTIE'S LUCK

Quacky was surprised when Mr. MacDougall gave him three dollars anyway.

He rode the elevator back down to street level and was glad to find Tennis Harper waiting outside for him. His other friends had to go home for various reasons, but Tennis said he would stick around a while.

"Let's go to Riverland," Quacky suggested.

As they biked to the amusement park, Quacky told Tennis about Felix Morgnester and his visit there earlier that day.

"I promised I'd give him the three dollars," Quacky explained.

They pedaled south again and, after a while, reached Riverland. As usual, it was deserted and eerie-looking, even in the sunlight that shone between the dark afternoon clouds.

"So, the voices and barking we heard yesterday could have been something or someone else," Quacky concluded as they locked their bikes together again outside Aladdin's Castle. "Felix said he wasn't there when we were yesterday."

Quacky led the way up the stairs and inside Aladdin's mouth. It was becoming old stuff to him, and he was no longer as apprehensive as he had been earlier. But still he felt someone's eyes on him and mentioned it to Tennis.

"Maybe it's Felix Morgnester," Tennis suggested.

"Well, it couldn't have been him yesterday, when I felt someone staring at me," Quacky reminded him.

"So, you've come back."

Startled, Quacky and Tennis turned around just as they entered the entrance hall. They held their breath.

Felix Morgnester stood behind them, at the castle entrance. He seemed more sinister than he had earlier, Quacky thought. Something about him troubled Quacky. Was it because he wondered now if Felix *was* playing with a full deck of cards? Facing a man who might be crazy no longer sounded funny to Quacky.

Was *Felix* the dognapper?, Quacky wondered. That would be one way of making a living, he realized. Steal people's dogs and cats, and collect the ransom money.

"We came back to give you the three dollars I promised," Quacky explained, hoping he sounded convincing. The way Felix was looking at him now, Quacky feared that the old man was losing patience with him. Quacky remembered he had already been warned to stay away from the park and the castle.

"You didn't tell the police on me, did you?" Felix asked, frowning with intense gray eyes. His clothes looked older and more wrinkled to Quacky. His face looked meaner.

"No!" Quacky told him emphatically. "I just walked the lady's cat, like I told you." He held out the three dollars for Felix.

I *did* tell him I was going to walk a cat for three dollars, Quacky realized. Felix knew about the cat; he might also have known who owned the cat. Mrs. MacDougall could afford to pay a big ransom for Jennifer-Louise. Maybe Felix knew that, too.

Felix looked at the three dollars and then at Quacky. He snatched the money out of Quacky's hand and stuffed it into one of his pants pockets.

"Now you boys better be going," Felix almost snarled at them. "Like I told you this morning...this isn't a safe place to hang around."

"Loose boards," Quacky told Tennis. But he was thinking that Felix meant the park and castle weren't safe for other reasons.

"Yeah. So you'd better go now."

Quacky looked at Tennis and hesitated.

"Maybe you could tell us something about the park, before we go?" Quacky asked Felix.

"I don't know anything about this place," Felix grumbled. He put his left hand on Quacky's back and his right on Tennis's and almost pushed them out through Aladdin's mouth to the daylight outside.

Quacky was about to argue with him and remind Felix that, in the old days, Felix had been a carny barker at Riverland. But he could tell Felix was in no mood to talk about all that now.

As Quacky and Tennis unlocked their bikes and began to ride out of the park, they looked back and saw that Felix was standing watching them from Aladdin's mouth.

"Wonder what's eating him?" Quacky asked. "He wasn't as uptight as that this morning. He seemed sort of friendly then."

"He sure isn't friendly now," Tennis assured Quacky. "I think if we had tried to stay and look around, he'd have beaned us with something."

"He's up to something there, I've got a feeling," Quacky told his friend. "And he's not the only one living there."

"You think maybe *he* stole the cat, and Puddles and the others?"

Quacky looked at Tennis as they both pedaled away from the old amusement park.

"What do you think went wrong?" Quacky asked Jerry later, at the mortuary. He had decided to make a clean breast of it to Jerry, about going back to Riverland and talking again to Felix Morgnester.

"The wrong person took the book," Jerry explained simply. "The kid got to it before the dognapper could. But, Quacky, I asked you not to go back to Riverland anymore, and you went ahead and did it. I thought we were pals, and you'd do what I asked if I thought it was right for you?"

Quacky could only say he was sorry.

"But I've got to find out about Riverland, for my Social Studies assignment," he pleaded, hoping to find an excuse for Jerry to say he could go back there again.

"You can find stuff about it in the library, in old newspaper articles or something," Jerry advised him. "I'm not going to tell you not to go there again, Quacky, because I don't like people giving me orders and cramping my style, and I figure you don't like it either. All I want you to do is play fair with me. If you do go there again, and I hope you won't, I want you to let me know. At least then, if anything happens to you there, I can come after you."

He's really worried something will happen to me at Riverland, Quacky realized. Well, I'll be careful, and I'll let him know I'm going there, if I can. It was good, he thought, having Jerry around and looking after him like a father. He had been waiting for someone to care about him like that for a long time. Someone besides Aunt Maggie. A man to care the way she cared. A man who would be his father.

Jerry wasn't like his Uncle Otis, Quacky knew. They both were men who had wandered a lot. But Jerry liked staying at Aunt Maggie's and being with Quacky. He wanted to be part of a family now. Uncle Otis still couldn't settle into a home life, Quacky supposed. He would stay around a while, then vanish.

Quacky thought it was odd. All the other old people he knew, from Aunt Maggie to Mattie Mayflower, and from Morton Horton and the other former house guests to Felix Morgnester himself . . . they all seemed to want to have a home and be part of a family. All except Uncle Otis.

Well, it takes all kinds of people to make up a world, he thought. He left Jerry then, figuring he was really lucky that Jerry wasn't a bit like his Uncle Otis.

When he rode his bike over to Mattie Mayflower's to see how Aunt Maggie was doing with her that afternoon, Quacky spotted a blank white envelope just inside the Mayflower gate. He hurried up to the second floor of the Mayflower house with the envelope.

Aunt Maggie was just coming out of Mattie's bedroom and met him in the hall. "Shh," she told Quacky. "She's asleep. The doctor came back and gave her something to help her sleep. He says her left side is just bruised and sprained. She'll be all right, but she has to stay in bed a few days or a week."

Quacky didn't say anything until they had gone downstairs together. Then he held out the envelope.

"Oh, not another one of those things!" Aunt Maggie exclaimed. She tore open the envelope, and Quacky read it aloud:

"You dummies! You put the dough in the wrong book! *The Call of the Wild* I looked in was upstairs on the Juvenile shelf, not downstairs on the Adult shelf!

"I saw you kids following that boy out of the library after I took the kitten. I thought you botched things up, so I went in and had somebody ask if that kid checked out *The Call of the Wild*. When the librarian said he had, I knew you'd goofed. Now we got to set up another way to operate a trade. You rich people don't care how you throw your money around, letting the wrong person get the money! Now get it *right* next time!"

Quacky and Aunt Maggie looked at each other in wonder. That was all the note said. It did not say what the dognapper-catnapper was going to do next.

"This time, Quacky, I think you'd better let the police handle things," Aunt Maggie suggested. It was more like an order than a suggestion, he thought.

But he was getting pretty impatient for results. He missed Puddles more all the time and wanted him back. He made up his mind that if the police didn't work faster, he'd beat them to finding Puddles, Pattie, Jennifer-Louise, and all the rest.

"The thing for us to do," he told Tennis on the phone later, "is to go to Riverland at *night*. If Felix *is* the dog-catnapper, we'll be able to sneak into Aladdin's Castle at night and look around and catch him with the goods."

It was a good idea, Tennis had to admit. But Quacky could tell his friend was not very anxious to go there after dark.

"I know what!" Quacky cried. "We'll get Ralph and Will and Katie to come with us! How about tonight, after dark?"

"I can't go tonight," Tennis replied. "My folks are playing in a tournament tonight, and I've got to sit with . . . ."

"I know, you've got to sit with Backhand." Quacky was very disappointed. At first he thought they could take Backhand with them.

But then he remembered what had happened to Jennifer-Louise when he tried taking her along on his business. He figured he'd better not take any chances with a baby girl. "Tomorrow night, then. That might be even better. It's Halloween!"

"We couldn't pick a spookier place to go on Halloween!" Tennis agreed. "Okay, I'll psych myself up for it somehow, and maybe with all of us together in Aladdin's Castle, we'll come out alive!"

Quacky could hardly wait. The only thing he wasn't certain about now was what costume to wear.

Without telling Jerry where he planned to go on Halloween, Quacky asked his advice when Jerry came home from work that night. He needed a costume that, if necessary, could scare a ghost.

"I put something great together once for Halloween when I was your age, Quacky," Jerry told him. "I think I can work you up into the outfit and, I guarantee, you'll knock 'em dead!"

Just what I want to do, Quacky thought to himself.

Later that Saturday night, Aunt Maggie brought Quacky along with her to Mattie Mayflower's house, so both of them could keep the old lady company. Quacky carried along his

Monopoly game with him and made some stand-in fifty-dollar bills to take the place of those he had lost in the ransom payment foul-up.

It began to rain again while they were sitting in Mattie's bedroom, and as Quacky listened to the downpour he could see that even Aunt Maggie thought it was a pretty spooky house to be in at night, especially in another thunderstorm. He wished they had been able to talk Jerry into coming with them, but Jerry had a date that night with Lieutenant O'Rourke. He took her to a movie, but only after he managed to convince her that it was too late on a rainy night for her to catch a dognapper. Chief Dooley had put her in charge of the investigation.

As thunder rolled overhead and lightning streaked and flashed, Quacky set up the Monopoly game on a board by Mattie Mayflower's bed. She was feeling better and said she would play a while, to take her mind off how much she was missing Pattie. Aunt Maggie didn't join them. She was busy writing her astrology column for the *Smedley Gazette*, working at a writing table in Mattie's bedroom.

"Do the stars say Pattie will be back soon?" Mattie asked her.

"I don't know Pattie's birth chart," Aunt Maggie told her. "Do you know when and where she was born?"

"No, I'm afraid she was a stray," Mattie ad-

DEL ROBLE SCHOOL LIBRARY

mitted. "She wandered into my yard one day and stayed."

Another orphan, Quacky thought. No wonder he liked Pattie, and Puddles liked her, too. They were *three* peas in a pod.

"Maybe you can tell from *my* birth chart," Mattie suggested.

Quacky laughed, knowing how little encouragement Aunt Maggie needed to make up a horoscope on somebody. But that would be swell, he thought suddenly. If she makes up a birth chart on Miss Mayflower, I can learn a lot more about her! Too bad Ralph isn't here, he thought, but he knew how unlikely that would be, on such a stormy night.

"I was born right here in this house," Mattie told Aunt Maggie. "On Christmas Eve, December 24, 1894."

Quacky had to think fast, to calculate if that was before the Civil War or after. It was only about thirty years after, he decided. No wonder she looks old. She *is* old! She's 87, he figured out.

Aunt Maggie apologized for not having any of her books with her, which she used to cast birth charts. But she was able to tell Mattie a few things about herself, just from her birth sign.

"You're a Capricorn," Aunt Maggie told her. "Capricorns are serious people. Everything they do has a purpose, and they hate to waste time."

"I was always busy, when I was younger," Mattie admitted. "I was Smedley's first librarian. I'll bet you didn't know that!"

Neither of them knew that, or anything else about her. Quacky listened with a keen ear. He was getting a lot more information about Miss Mayflower than he had ever thought he would. He would ask some leading questions later, about the house and the Mayflower family.

"Quacky, I can't do a good horoscope without my books," Aunt Maggie told him. "I know it's raining out, but . . . . "

"I'll go get them!" he volunteered. "Just don't do any more of her horoscope until I get back," he whispered to his aunt.

He ran home, got the books she asked for, and ran back with them safely dry under his raincoat. When he entered the yard again he saw another white envelope lying just inside the gate.

When he got back to Mattie Mayflower's room upstairs in the old house, he handed her the envelope. Once again, it was blank, but sealed.

"You open it, Maggie," Mattie told her, waiting anxiously. "I do hope it's good news this time, about Pattie."

Aunt Maggie opened the letter and gave it to

Quacky. He quickly peeled off his soaking wet raincoat and dropped it onto the floor before eagerly reading the new ransom note aloud:

"Dear Rich Lady—Your dog's run away on us! The male's still here, though. The price for him is only $500 now, like it was in the first place."

"Pattie's run away!" Quacky exclaimed.

Mattie Mayflower sat up more erectly in bed, looking better already.

"She'll come running home, I know she will!" Miss Mayflower declared.

Quacky couldn't help but wish it had been Puddles who escaped from the dognappers.

"Is there more?" Mattie asked Quacky.

Quacky looked back at the ransom note and read further:

"It says, 'Put the money in a bag, tomorrow night for Trick or Treat. Hang the bag with the money in it on the big old elm tree in Centennial Park before eight o'clock. If you treat us right with the ransom money, you'll get your dog back. But if you try to trick us, look out! You'll never see him again! AND DON'T CALL THE COPS!' "

Quacky found something in the note that surprised him.

"There must be more than one of them," he deducted. "This is the first time the dognapper used the word 'us.' I kept thinking there was just one dognapper."

"More reason than ever to let the police handle it," Aunt Maggie told him. "Soon as we get home, I'll call the police about it. Lieutenant O'Rourke ought to know about this as soon as possible."

"Please, Aunt Maggie," Quacky pleaded. "If the police are called in, I might *never* get Puddles back!"

Aunt Maggie relented and said they would discuss it later.

"What else can you tell me about my horoscope?" Mattie asked. "Does it say Pattie will be back home right away?"

Aunt Maggie looked up dates in her ephemeris, a book that told where the stars were at specific times and places through the years. Soon, she had Mattie's horoscope completed.

"It's a very interesting birth chart," Aunt Maggie reported, studying it closely. "For one thing, when Capricorns are young, they prefer friends who are older. When they are old, they like to be around young people."

Mattie gave Quacky a look that told him that's how she felt about him.

"Capricorns are generous and kind," Aunt Maggie continued. "They're very willing to lend help whenever it's needed."

"I used to volunteer for everything," Mattie admitted. "I worked for the Red Cross and helped organize the March of Dimes in Smedley, to fight polio."

"A typical Capricorn is of medium height or smaller," Aunt Maggie said as she and Quacky looked at the old woman. "They tend to be rather bony, since Capricorn rules the bones."

"That's me, just an old bag of bones," Mattie laughed. "Might hang me up tomorrow night for Halloween, and use me for a skeleton!"

Quacky laughed and shuddered all at the same time.

"Capricorns want security and they like to be famous and well-respected," Aunt Maggie went on. "Forgive me, Mattie, but Capricorns often want to be the biggest fish in their pond."

Mattie had to laugh. "That's me, all right. That's probably why I never married. No man could stand me, I was so proud and stubborn and wanted things my own way. But then, that was back when men ruled the roost more than women let them, today. I guess I was just a 'women's libber' a ways before its time!"

Quacky was finding it all very interesting. He didn't think he'd forget any of it, he was listening so hard.

"As for security, that's true about me, too. This house has been my security. The family money went, a long time ago. But even though I found it hard to pay the mortgage and taxes, I kept going. That's where I've been going every night all these years."

Quacky and Aunt Maggie looked at her, wondering what she meant about her nocturnal outings.

"You thought I was just going out grocery-shopping or something," she told Quacky. "No, I've been going out to work at night."

"Working? At 87?" Aunt Maggie gasped. "What are you, a disco dancer?"

"Close," Mattie confided, a teasing grin on her wrinkled face.

Quacky could hardly wait for her to explain.

"I was always good at cards. My father taught me to play poker. He won more money playing poker in his lifetime than he ever did managing the Mayflower Candy Company."

"Mayflower candies!" Quacky cried. "I remember them! Aunt Maggie, you used to tell me how delicious the fudge was. Miss Mayflower, did your company make licorice?"

"We made some of the finest licorice anywhere," Mattie boasted.

"Too bad you don't make it now," Quacky said. "My friend Jerry loves licorice. He likes it heated and scorched, and then left to get cold and brittle."

"We never did that to our licorice, but I suppose your friend knows what he likes."

"I like it too, I guess." Quacky thought it over. "I had some a while back, but I like it fresh and limpy better, so you can tear it off with your teeth."

"The candy company closed years ago," Mattie said, deep in memories. "But even after we gave up the business, Father made money all the time, playing poker and winning. He taught me everything he knew about the game. I play for the house, at the Country Club, almost every night. They don't pay me much, but I do get to eat with the help in the kitchen afterward."

No wonder you never came out of your house during the daytime!, Quacky realized. You work all night, and sleep all day!

"Gambling isn't in your Capricorn chart," Aunt Maggie told Mattie. "But you also have a lot of Sagittarius. They're very lucky people, though they seldom become rich."

"That's certainly me!" Mattie confessed.

"And Sagittarians make good librarians, among other things, such as horse trainers and jockeys and other athletes," Aunt Maggie added.

"I always loved to ride horses," Mattie remembered. "I think that's why the beau I liked best of all never proposed to me. He was afraid of horses, and I rode so well. Now it seems to me like a silly, inconsequential thing to keep us from getting married. But that's probably why most people don't see eye-to-eye enough to marry. Over the silly, little things."

Quacky could see that Mattie Mayflower had reminded his Aunt Maggie of Otis and herself. The "little thing" they had fallen out over, time and time again, he figured, was settling down to married life and its routine. He hoped his Uncle Otis would come around on that some-time soon and come back to them. He was glad, though, to think that Jerry seemed to like being around them more and more.

Maybe tonight, right now, Jerry is proposing to Lieutenant O'Rourke, Quacky thought. Maybe they'll get married and adopt me! He had been hoping for that a lot lately. Almost as much as he kept hoping Puddles would come back home to him.

"Your birth chart *does* say you're lucky, Mattie," Aunt Maggie promised her. "So Pattie is bound to turn up, sooner than later."

"What was that?" Mattie was listening in-tently to something Aunt Maggie and Quacky hadn't heard.

"I just said . . . . "

Mattie shushed Aunt Maggie as politely as she could, and they all listened.

A whimpering sound came from somewhere outside the bedroom.

They all looked to the doorway and, mo-ments later, saw a tired, panting, scared dog enter the room, soaking wet.

10

A NEW TRAP
IS SET

"I'll bet you know where Puddles is," Quacky told Pattie, toweling her dry quickly so she could be lifted onto the bed and into Mattie Mayflower's eager arms.

He wished he could take Pattie out again, right then, and have her lead him to Puddles, wherever he was being held prisoner. He looked at Pattie closely, for any sign of where she had been, but he found nothing.

"She doesn't look mistreated, just wet and scared," Mattie said, looking Pattie over as she held her, so relieved she was almost in tears. "Oh, Quacky, I hope you find Puddles soon. Maybe he's home now, waiting for you!"

Quacky hadn't thought of that. He looked at

Aunt Maggie, and her eyes told him he could run right home and see.

Quacky ran out of the room and down the stairs, as fast as he could. In his haste, he forgot to take his raincoat, but didn't mind how wet he would get. He might find Puddles waiting for him at home!

Through the rain he ran, down the block toward home. But as he approached the house and looked hard at the front door, he didn't see Puddles. No one was there. It was just raining, very hard, on the doorstep.

He looked all around the front yard, but did not find Puddles. Just then, Jerry drove up in Aunt Maggie's old car.

"What are you doing getting drowned out here?" Jerry asked.

He parked the car and got out, hurrying to take Quacky inside the house with him. Quacky told him about Pattie and explained what he had hoped. Jerry shook his head.

"Tough luck, pal," Jerry said, trying to comfort him. "But it won't help you find Puddles if you come down with a bad cold."

Quacky started sneezing, in sixes as he always did, and Jerry looked at him as if his prediction had already come true. Jerry put a hand on Quacky's wet forehead and nodded.

"Just what I was afraid of, Quacky. You've caught a nasty cold already, from chasing around so much and being out in the rain. You're going right up to bed!"

After Quacky grudgingly took a hot bath, got into his pajamas, and climbed into bed, Jerry drove over to Miss Mayflower's, to bring Aunt Maggie home.

Once back home, Aunt Maggie took a look at Quacky and stuck a thermometer in his mouth.

"You've been upset about Puddles, and chasing around who knows where, trying to find him," she complained. When she took the thermometer out of his mouth and read it, she shook her head. "You've got a fever, so you'll have to rest in bed until it comes down and your cold gets better."

"But what about Halloween tomorrow night, and finding Puddles?" Quacky wailed and then coughed as Aunt Maggie began rubbing a smelly salve on his chest.

"You just forget about all that for a while," she ordered. "We'll see that you don't miss out on Halloween, and you'll get Puddles back. Won't he, Jerry?"

"Sure, Quacky," Jerry tried to convince him. "You just get some rest. Sally says Mister Mac-Dougall got a ransom note for his wife's cat. The catnapper's demanding $500 for her. You can bet the police will go into high gear now, with MacDougall's wife waiting to get her cat back."

Quacky coughed some more, then told Jerry

about the latest ransom note Mattie got, telling her to put $500 in a bag and hang it from the old elm tree by eight o'clock Halloween night in Centennial Park.

"Promise you won't tell Sally, or any of the other police about it?" Quacky asked anxiously from his bed. "The ransom note said 'Don't call the cops' or I'll never see Puddles again."

Reluctantly, Jerry agreed and Quacky rested his head back on his pillow. Just before they left his room, he sat up again and sneezed six more times.

Quacky awoke in the middle of the night. Lions and tigers had been chasing him through the room with the cages in Aladdin's Castle. They ran after him as he crawled on his hands and knees through the barrel room, the walls, ceiling, and floor turning and spinning him like a rock in a polishing tumbler.

Dogs and cats, hundreds of them, began chasing after the lions and tigers, who were just about to get Quacky. Then he fell down the chute, and they all fell after him, tail over nose, down, down, down.

He sat bolt upright in bed and looked around, feeling feverish.

It was only a nightmare, he realized. When he lay his head back on his pillow, he could only think of one thing. How much he missed Puddles.

"I haven't been trying hard enough, Puddles," he said, looking at the large unlidded cardboard box beside his bed where Puddles always slept on an old throw rug. Puddles hated a regular dog bed and would only sleep in the old cardboard box that someone's air conditioner had come in. Quacky had found it outside an appliance shop, and it fit Puddles a little on the tight side. But Puddles liked to walk around inside the box four times in a circle, then plop down in a ball, and look at Quacky with big brown eyes before they both fell off to sleep.

In the darkened room, Quacky pretended Puddles was all curled up in his usual ball in the box, asleep. Finally, Quacky fell asleep again, this time not to wake until morning.

Aunt Maggie served him a light breakfast on a tray in bed. Orange juice, half a grapefruit, and some hot tea with honey in it. No aspirin, because she didn't believe in using aspirin or any other drug. She ordered him to stay in bed all day and nap as much as he could, while she looked in on Mattie Mayflower again.

It was Sunday morning, but Jerry was needed at the mortuary to help get two funerals ready for Monday.

"If you get out of that bed before I get home later, except to go to the john or the refrigerator, I'm gonna box your ears!" Jerry threatened. "I'll bring you as many new science-fiction comic books as I can find. And when you're better, we'll go see a sci-fi movie if there are any in town, all right?"

Quacky was starting to feel better already.

Ralph came to visit with Clemontis Regis after a while.

"What are you going to dress up as, for tonight?" Quacky asked from bed.

"Spiderman, I guess," Ralph thought. "Mom bought me the costume, from the dime store. How about you? You getting out of bed for the big bonfire in Centennial Park tonight and for Trick or Treating?"

"Heck, yeah. I'll talk 'em into letting me, don't worry."

"What are you going to dress up in?" Ralph asked, trying to keep Clemontis from jumping on Quacky's bed and crushing him to death.

"Jerry's got some idea for my costume. Won't tell me what it is. But he says it'll be mighty scary."

While Ralph was there, Quacky told him everything he had learned about Mattie Mayflower and her house, the night before.

"Sounds like enough right now, for my report," Ralph said happily, then thanked Quacky for his help and left.

Even though he tried not to, Quacky kept falling asleep. He figured it was his cold, making him take it easy. But he didn't mind. He was going to get of bed that night, to go Trick

or Treating in his scary costume, and he was
going to find Puddles. Somehow he had the no-
tion that he *was* going to find his dog on Halloween night.

"Pattie has a cold, too," Aunt Maggie told
Quacky when she looked in on him that afternoon. "She must have come a long way in the
rain last night."

"Have you heard from your friends yet?" he
asked.

"No, but I suppose they're getting settled in,
wherever they went," she replied. "I just wonder where they could have gone. I don't think
that the four of them have enough money together to buy a good dinner, much less rent an
apartment big enough for all of them. They
weren't any sort of 'burden' on us, were they,
Quacky?"

"Heck no! I was getting a kick out of Horton
and Norton," Quacky said, then coughed and
sneezed six more times. Taking a deep breath,
he told her about the to-do over the disco
shoes in the police station that Friday, and she
shook her head.

"Well, I guess men will be men!" she declared.

When Quacky awakened later from another
nap, he saw it was already dark outside his
window. Days when you're sick with a cold
are unlike any other days, Quacky concluded.
They put you in a sort of never-never land.

Maybe it's because a cold makes you feel groggy or dopey.

Sounds from outside the house seem as if they're coming from the moon, he thought. Every sound is strange and faraway. Every time he heard a dog bark, even though he knew it wasn't Puddles's bark, he expected Puddles to come into his room and jump up on his bed, and half drown him with wet kisses.

He felt better now and got out of bed, but didn't go either to the bathroom or the kitchen. He went to the window and looked out.

It had stopped raining, but it looked like a typical Halloween night. Dark and blustery. The wind was blowing the almost bare tree branches, and they were beating against the side of the house and each other.

A spooky night, he thought. A great night for a bonfire and prowling around town in a scary outfit. He already knew where he would wind up that night with his friends. He could hardly wait to get into costume and get there!

When he heard the front door open, he started down the stairs in his pajamas and slippers, and saw that it was Jerry.

"Here are the comic books," Jerry told him, waving them over his head. "How're you feeling?"

"Lots better, really," Quacky lied, trying not to cough or sneeze. "Jerry, I don't want to miss out on Halloween."

"You won't miss out on it," Jerry assured him, meeting him on the stairs and feeling his forehead. "Hey, I think you've licked your fever."

"What's in the big paper bag?" Quacky asked, curious at the bag Jerry had under one arm.

"Up to your room, now," Jerry ordered. "Time to put on your costume!"

Quacky turned on the stairs and hurried back to his room as Jerry came in behind him and put the bag on the bed.

"Found it by luck, in a second-hand store. Made the owner open up so I could look, even though it's Sunday!" Jerry pulled a black woolen turtleneck sweater out of the bag and held it up proudly against Quacky's chest. "It has to be a little big," he explained.

Quacky thought he could fit himself and Tennis Harper and maybe even Will Kelly inside the sweater, and wondered what it had to do with a scary Halloween costume.

"Give me that pillow on your bed, Quacky," Jerry asked him.

Quacky handed Jerry his pillow and watched as Jerry took some string out of his pants pocket. Quacky stood patiently while Jerry went to work on him.

Jerry tied the pillow to Quacky's back by

crossing the string several times around his chest, right over his pajama top.

"Now get into some jeans," Jerry urged him. "Right over the pajama pants, so you'll be warmer outside tonight."

Quacky obeyed quickly, relieved to hear that he was going to be allowed out after all. He knew he could trust Jerry not to let him down.

"Now we'll just pull this turtleneck sweater over your head," Jerry said after Quacky got into his Levi's and closed the belt.

The sweater went over Quacky's head and the pillow on his back, and Jerry adjusted the sleeves by rolling them up at the cuff twice and at the waist once.

"Now bend a little at the waist and go to the full-length mirror in the john," Jerry told him.

Quacky bent over and walked that way to the mirror on the bathroom wall and was amazed at what he saw.

"The Hunchback of Notre Dame!" Quacky exclaimed happily. "I don't believe it, Jerry! What a great costume!"

"No mask, no nothing else. Just look and walk like the old Hunchback of Notre Dame. You'll scare everybody! I did it once when I was your age and nobody could beat it."

Quacky practiced walking around the bedroom like Quasimodo, the scary hunchback in the famous French novel. He had seen the movie on television once, with Charles Laughton playing the hunchback, and could hardly get to sleep that night.

Quacky wrinkled up his face, swung his arms in front of himself, apelike, and moved a little sideways as he walked forward, moving somewhat like a dog.

"You've got it, Quacky!" Jerry convinced him. "Go around just like that, and you'll knock 'em out!"

"Now what about the ransom payment for the old elm tree tonight?" Quacky asked.

"Don't worry about that, Quacky," Jerry told him. "Aunt Maggie and I will put something in a bag and hang it on the tree. The bonfire is going to be lighted at eight o'clock sharp. The dognapper must figure there'll be too many people around for him to get caught taking the ransom money."

"Then you're going to catch the dognapper?"

"I'm gonna try."

Quacky felt a lot better already, knowing Jerry was going to lay a trap for the dognapper.

"You and your friends just have fun tonight," Jerry said. "You'll have Puddles back home tonight or I won't come home until I find him!"

The doorbell rang and Aunt Maggie, who had just come home, answered it. Katie and Tennis were just putting on their masks as they stood on the doorstep. Will came up the walk just as Ralph was walking over from next door.

Aunt Maggie let Quacky's friends into the house as Jerry called down to her.

"His fever's gone. You said he could go out tonight if he felt better."

"All right," Aunt Maggie called up the stairs. "But, Quacky, don't tire yourself out tonight. And if it rains again, go somewhere to stay dry."

"Come on down, Quacky!" Tennis cried from the foot of the stairs, adjusting the jacket of his bum's outfit, his face smudged with dirt. "Ralph says you've got a real scary costume."

Quacky hurried to get a pillow case to hold all the treats he expected to collect that night. Holding the case in one hand, he began moving forward and a little sideways, bent over with his arms swinging apelike in front of him as he lumbered down the stairs while all of his friends watched.

Katie gave out a cross between a scream and a squeal.

"You look like a real hunchback!" Tennis declared.

Quacky saw that Katie had blood all over her face and arms. She wore a torn old dress and her arms and legs were bandaged, as if she had been in a terrible accident. He sniffed and examined her arms and discovered she was really only spattered with ketchup.

Ralph was dressed as Spiderman. Will Kelly was almost completely disguised in a bed sheet with two holes for his eyes. Will began making high-pitched spooky sounds, as if he were a Space Age ghost.

"Trick or Treat!" Quacky challenged Aunt Maggie, startling her as she came into the parlor from the kitchen.

"Quacky!" she cried, holding her throat. "I thought a monster had gotten into the house!"

"Trick or Treat!" he repeated, moving on her menacingly.

"Stay back!" she pleaded. "I've brought some treats." She gave each one some bubblegum and pennies. "Now be careful what treats you get."

As Quacky and his friends left the house and started up the walk, Aunt Maggie and Jerry stood in the doorway. When she saw they all had their bicycles with them, she called out, "Trick or Treating on bicycles?"

"So we can get to Centennial Park," Quacky explained. He hoped it would satisfy her as the reason for taking their bicycles along. He knew they would be needing them if they wound up that night where he expected them to go.

He was glad when Aunt Maggie seemed to accept his explanation.

"There's a full moon out," she called to him as Quacky and his pals began moving up the block, walking their bikes with their treat bags in their bicycle baskets. "A lot of weird things happen under a full moon. Especially on Halloween. Look out for spooks and werewolves!"

Quacky began looking over his shoulder.

11

SPOOKS
ON THE LOOSE

Quacky led them first to Mattie Mayflower's house.

"Aren't you afraid to come here anymore?" Ralph asked him as they all stood outside the big iron gate. Dark clouds hung over the old house, and shadows fell everywhere about them.

"It sure looks spooky," Katie admitted.

"Almost as spooky as Aladdin's Castle!" Tennis agreed.

"Later, let's go there!" Quacky suggested.

"On Halloween night, with a full moon out?" Will's eyes opened wide in the holes of his ghostly bed sheet.

"You should be the least afraid," Quacky

turned to him and laughed. "You're a ghost!"

"Are we really going to go to Riverland tonight?" Tennis asked Quacky as he followed him through the gate and up the walk, the others close behind.

"Maybe, if Jerry's plan doesn't work. But I want to ask Miss Mayflower a favor, first."

Quacky explained at the front door that the bell didn't ring, and Miss Mayflower couldn't answer their knock because she was upstairs in bed. He opened the door and called, "Miss Mayflower, it's Quacky," so he wouldn't frighten her.

He didn't expect her to yell back down to him all that way from her bedroom, so he just led his friends up the winding stairway to the second floor and poked his head in on her. He saw her sitting up in bed in her nightgown, a nightcap on her head.

"Don't be scared, Miss Mayflower," he cautioned her before entering her room. "I'm dressed up as a hunchback, for Halloween, and I've brought some friends to meet you. They're in costume, too. Your chart says you like young people, remember?"

"Come right in, Quacky," she welcomed him. "And your friends, too. Oh, I see Ralph is with you. Hello, Ralph."

Quacky introduced her to Katie, Tennis, and Will, and she apologized for not having any treats for them.

"In the old days, when we had the candy company, we gave out lots of nice treats on Halloween," Miss Mayflower recalled. "You won't play a trick on me if I don't have any treats for you, will you?"

"No, but I've come to ask a favor," Quacky told her anxiously.

"Of course, Quacky. What can I do for you?"

He looked around the room, but did not see Pattie.

"Pattie hasn't run off again has she?" he asked, worried.

"No, she's probably under the bed. I think she's a little afraid of all of you."

Quacky got onto his knees and found Pattie cowering nervously under the old woman's bed. He scratched her gently behind the ears, which he knew Puddles loved, and coaxed the dog out.

"The favor is, I'd like to sort of borrow Pattie, for just a few hours tonight." Quacky held his breath, waiting for Miss Mayflower to say yes or no. Before she could answer, he thought he should explain. "I think she could lead me to Puddles. I'll take very good care of her, I promise."

The old lady looked as if giving up Pattie, even for just a few hours, was just about the last favor she could grant Quacky.

"Very well, Quacky," she relented. "I know you'll bring her back safely later. You miss your dog very much, just as I missed Pattie. If I can help you in any way to get Puddles back, I will. Go ahead now, and good luck. But *do* bring her back as soon as you can?"

"I will, I promise," Quacky assured her and led Pattie away, to take her along. The dog seemed eager to be off on another prowl, now that she had become friends with Quacky.

They had left their bikes in Mattie Mayflower's yard and got them again to start out on their rounds of Trick or Treat, now joined by Pattie. Quacky thought they made a weird sight, all in costume and riding bikes, especially Will. He had never seen a ghost riding a bicycle before. Pattie kept barking at Will.

All the while they Trick-or-Treated, Quacky worried that Jerry might call the police after all, to trap the dognapper. He felt guilty for thinking Jerry might go back on his word, but he still worried that Jerry would tell Lieutenant O'Rourke.

He just didn't have his mind on Trick-or-Treating, as he usually did on Halloween. Every time he looked down at Pattie, following close at their heels as they went from house to house and block to block, he thought of Puddles and missed him more and more.

And he was concentrating on a new plan developing in his head. He was becoming more certain all the time that Pattie could help lead him to Puddles, if necessary.

As eight o'clock approached, Quacky led his pals on a bike race over to Centennial Park, Pattie running after them and barking excitedly.

The park was a square block of trees, bushes, flowers, and some benches in the heart of Smedley. A plaque stated that it had been dedicated in 1948 for the town's 100th anniversary.

Mobs of people, mostly children in costume, were crowded into the park. Quacky thought he got more than his share of startled looks. To add to the realism of his hunchback outfit, he panted and grunted.

Quacky didn't move around as the scary hunchback for nothing. Part of his plan was to check out the old elm tree that was a landmark of the park. It was supposed to be the oldest tree in the county.

He saw a small cloth sack hanging from a branch he would have to stand on tiptoes to reach. Jerry had hung it there, he figured. As casually as he could, he cautioned all his pals not to look at it at the same time, but to take turns watching the sack. He asked them to keep checking on it, as they too moved around the park, so they could see who would take it.

Quacky didn't think the dognapper had made a very good plan. Just like putting the money in a library book, he thought. It wasn't foolproof. What if somebody else saw the sack hanging from the tree? They might get the $500 before the dognapper did!

Well, even if the wrong person does get the sack, there won't be any real money in it, Quacky was certain. Jerry wouldn't take any chances like that!

And no matter who took the money sack, Quacky was sure the dognapper would get caught, this time. If the wrong person got the money, the dognapper was sure to be watching. Quacky and his pals would notice how mad the dognapper would be acting, and when he left the park, they would follow him to where Puddles was being held prisoner.

"Light the bonfire!" someone shouted, and Quacky knew it must be eight o'clock.

Some men were standing around a small mountain of wood and old furniture. They began tossing lighted matches onto it, and the police ordered people to stay back as the bonfire ignited and flames began roaring upward and sparks began flying. It was the biggest bonfire Quacky had ever seen, and he could hardly take his eyes off it. Still, he kept glancing away, to see if the money sack was still hanging from the old elm tree. Every time he looked, it was still there.

He worried that there were too many police officers in the park, but he understood they were there to make sure no one got hurt from the bonfire. They didn't know about the ran-

som money in the old tree, he was certain. He
just hoped that when things started happening,
the police in the park wouldn't scare off the
dognapper. He reasoned that the dognapper
had to expect police to be in the park that
night, to control the crowd and keep kids away
from the fire.

Katie and Tennis were helping him the most,
Quacky saw. They seemed to take turns with
him, checking on the sack in the tree. Ralph
and Will seemed to be hypnotized by the roaring fire.

The fire reached some wood that made it
spark and flame up even more, and everyone
yelled louder, in surprise and excitement, startling Pattie. She started to run away, but
Quacky raced after her and caught her.

Katie and Tennis turned to watch Pattie, too,
and suddenly Quacky realized that none of
them was watching the money sack. Holding
Pattie securely, Quacky looked behind him.

"It's gone!" he cried. "The sack's gone!"

He ran toward the elm, with Pattie and his
friends close behind. Quacky expected to see
Jerry, but he wasn't there. Pulling at his pillow,
which had slipped lower down his back, he
looked around quickly for any sign of a com-
motion.

A man in a black suit, wearing a black mask,
was running toward the south exit of the park,
the money sack in his hand. A tall witch and a

strong-looking magician in a flowing black cape were racing at his heels.

"After them!" Quacky commanded Pattie, starting to give chase. She ran after Quacky. His friends ran as hard as they could after them.

"Sic 'em, Pattie!" Quacky yelled to the dog, who was barking and growling at the three costumed runners just a few lengths ahead of them. She caught the magician's cape in her teeth, tripping him.

He fell to the grass like a ton of bricks and began clawing the ground with his hands.

Quacky made a flying leap and tackled the witch low around the legs, sending her crashing to the ground with a grunt and a howl.

The masked man was still racing away with the money sack.

"Go get the bum!" Quacky ordered Pattie, but the dog was too busy growling and barking at the magician she had downed.

Quacky got to his feet and yelled for Tennis and Katie and the others to hold those two, while he ran after the masked man. He heard police whistles then, and in the confusion realized that he had no chance of gaining on the dognapper, although he kept running as fast as he could, in spite of the pillow slipping lower and lower down his back.

Quacky saw a car pull up to the south exit of the park. The brakes screeched as it came to a sudden stop. The door next to the driver flew open, and the man with the money sack jumped inside just as the car roared off again, leaving an odor of burning rubber.

"After them!" Quacky yelled out, hoping police were nearby. "They're getting away!"

But when he looked around him, Quacky didn't see any police anywhere near. Helplessly, he stood and watched the getaway car and knew he couldn't even have caught up with it if he had been on his bicycle.

His shoulders dropping in despair, the hunchback pillow now resting around his bottom, Quacky walked dejectedly back to where his friends and Pattie were holding the witch and magician. He saw police now were gathered around them, and his hopes lifted again. The pair were the dognapper's accomplices, he was certain. They could still lead him to finding Puddles!

The witch, a tall woman in a long black dress with black gloves that went all the way up her skinny arms, was gasping for breath. She flailed her arms and told a policeman to keep his hands off her as he began to pull off her black mask. Pattie was barking and tearing apart the tall, black, cone-shaped witch's hat that had fallen off her head.

"Aunt Maggie!" Quacky exclaimed, as the witch's mask was removed.

Instantly fearing the worst, he looked at the magician, whose arms were being held behind him by one policeman as another one searched his black pants and black suitcoat.

A third policeman removed the magician's mask and made Quacky's worst fear come true.

"I guess I should have let you in on the trap," Jerry told Quacky.

12

DOORWAYS
TO MYSTERY

Quacky decided there was no time to waste.
While the police questioned Aunt Maggie and
Jerry, the dognappers were getting farther
away. He had to try *his* plan. Jerry's had failed.

"Quacky, come back here, and help us explain!" Aunt Maggie called to him as Quacky
began to run off with Pattie and his pals.

"You'll get out of it!" Quacky assured her.
"Here comes Lieutenant O'Rourke!"

"Follow that kid!" Jerry pleaded with the policemen holding and frisking him.

"He ain't done nothin'," one of the policemen told Jerry, letting Quacky and his friends
leave.

"Hey, what's going on over there?" Lieutenant O'Rourke called out, approaching the policemen holding Aunt Maggie and Jerry.

Quacky wanted to tell Jerry where he thought he was going now, with his friends. But he didn't want the police to know.

As soon as they left the park, Quacky stopped his friends, and he leaned over on his bike, patting Pattie gently on her head.

"Where is Puddles?" he asked.

At hearing Puddles's name, Pattie's ears stood up.

"She knows," Quacky told his pals. He looked back at the dog and commanded, "Pattie, take us to Puddles!"

The dog's tail began wagging and she panted excitedly. She turned her head and looked off to the south.

"Go, Pattie! Go find Puddles!" he urged her. "We'll follow!"

Pattie looked for a moment at Quacky. She barked shrilly and bolted off to the right of the park, down a street that led to the south side of town.

Quacky and his pals pedaled hard to keep up with Pattie as she ran faster and faster. They made a crazy sight, Quacky thought. A hunchback whose hump was sliding lower and lower; a bum; Spiderman; a bloody accident case; and a flowing ghost, all on bicycles, chasing after a wild dog!

After only a few blocks, Quacky was surer than ever where they were headed.

"She's taking us to Riverland!" he shouted over his shoulder to the others.

Less than fifteen minutes later, Quacky saw the roller-coaster tracks climbing high over the old amusement park. The cool night air blew dead leaves off the trees into a swirl around them as they approached. The park was as quiet as a cemetery, Quacky thought, except for a few plastic colored banners flapping in the breeze high atop dark lamp posts strung along the empty midway.

"What a spooky place to come to, on Halloween!" Katie shivered and looked around as they pulled their bikes through the opening in the high fence surrounding the park.

Soon they were riding their bikes up the deserted midway as Pattie headed toward Aladdin's Castle.

"Maybe we should go back and get the police?" Ralph suggested.

"This calls for an undercover job, Ralph," Quacky told him as he caught up with Pattie, just before she reached the castle.

Quacky got off his bike and held Pattie for a moment, looking into her eyes.

"So the trail *does* lead to Aladdin's Castle, just as I suspected. But okay, Pattie. Don't bark anymore. We've got to be very quiet. Now, take us to Puddles!"

Pattie wagged her tail and looked happier than she had been all night. She bolted off toward the castle.

"Wait, Pattie!" Quacky called to her softly as Pattie began running up the castle stairs.

She stopped and turned at the top of the stairs, to look back at Quacky for just a moment. Then she vanished inside Aladdin's mouth.

They parked their bikes and Quacky led the way up the dark, unlighted stairs to the doorway that was Aladdin's mouth.

"It's a lot spookier than during the daytime," Tennis admitted in a hoarse whisper to Quacky. "But, at least, now I'm not so worried there are ghosts here."

"Unless the dognappers are ghosts," Quacky suggested, enjoying a chance to scare his pal.

"Maybe I ought to wait outside, and watch the bikes," Ralph offered.

"They'll be okay, Ralph," Quacky was certain. "Do you really want to stay out here all by yourself?"

Ralph thought it over only for a moment. Then he hurried after them as they entered the castle.

"Gosh, it's dark in here!" Will declared, forgetting to be cautious, as they were all huddled together in the small, dark entrance room.

"Quiet," Quacky whispered huskily.

"Is Pattie here?" Katie asked.

Quacky fumbled in his jeans pocket and pulled out a tiny pencil flashlight and flicked it on. The batteries were low, but the faint light it cast was some reassurance they could find their way in the dark. But after flashing the light in every direction, they saw no sign of Pattie.

"She probably went through this door over here," Quacky told them, beaming his light in that direction.

He pushed it and found that the door was already half open. He stepped through and into the big gray room with the animal cages painted on the walls. Moonlight was streaking into the room from a small skylight overhead. Quacky hadn't noticed the skylight before, when he had been there in the daytime.

"I'm sure glad these cages aren't filled with lions and tigers," Will said nervously.

Quacky looked behind him and almost laughed. All his friends looked scared to death, but he thought Ralph looked the most frightened.

"Now, everyone lean against this real cage over here at the end of the wall," Quacky told them.

They all put their shoulders against the real cage. Suddenly each one began to fall down a steep ramp, feet over head. When they stopped falling and looked up, they found themselves in the room with painted lions and tigers snarling at them from the walls. This time, Quacky noticed that a little moonlight was coming in from some small, square air holes high up on the walls.

"I bet I know where Pattie went next," Quacky whispered to Tennis.

While the others stared at the ferocious-looking wild animals, Quacky told them to push against the biggest lion painted over another wall.

They pushed and stumbled into the small wooden-barrel room.

"Tennis says it used to turn and tumble you when you tried to crawl through," Quacky explained. "But it's hard enough just to walk through, it's so small and curved into a circle. You get the feeling that everything's moving."

"Did you hear something?" Tennis asked.

Quacky listened, and the others looked at him and Tennis.

"Voices," Quacky said, softly. "This is where we heard voices that first time, remember?"

Tennis said he remembered.

Quacky led the group through the barrel and into the dungeon beyond. The room was darker than the others, but with Quacky's little flashlight they could make out the skeletons hanging from chains that were holding them to the big, gray, stone-block walls.

"Hey, there's a stretching rack over there!" Katie cried, louder than Quacky thought was safe.

"This is as far as I've ever gone," Tennis admitted to Quacky. "I've always taken the tunnel way out, through the big door next to the rack."

"I haven't gone any farther either," Quacky assured him. "But we haven't found Pattie yet. She's somewhere around here. What do you think? You want to go back out, through the tunnel?"

Tennis said he was game to go farther.

"Tennis and I will go on, and meet the rest of you outside, if you want," Quacky told the others.

"I think maybe I've had enough, it being Halloween and everything," Ralph admitted sheepishly, but relieved.

"I'm glad you said so," Will told him. "I'm ready to get out of here, too."

"I'll go with you guys," Katie said to Quacky and Tennis.

The friends parted company beside the medieval torture rack. After Ralph and Will went into the tunnel that would take them outside behind the castle, Quacky, Tennis, and Katie searched for another way out of the dungeon, trying to pick up Pattie's trail.

Quacky felt along the stone wall until he

found something he thought was a door. Quacky pushed against it, and the wall opened outward, revealing a flight of old wooden stairs.

"It goes back up somewhere," Quacky told his pals nervously.

They began gingerly ascending the stairs, Quacky in the lead, followed by Tennis and Katie, just as Quacky's dying flashlight gave out. They were left in a pitch-dark stairway.

Quacky reached out his hands and found that he could touch the wall on either side of him.

"It's sure narrow," he whispered down to the others behind him. "I can't see a thing, the higher I climb."

He thought he had climbed enough stairs to reach the second floor of the castle. One of the steps was loose, and he nearly put his right foot through it. Quietly he warned Tennis and Katie.

Finally he reached a small landing that he could stand up on. But it was pitch dark where he stood, and he wondered where a door might be.

He heard a whining sound.

"I think I hear Pattie, on the other side of a door somewhere up here," Quacky told them as his pals joined him and huddled on the small landing at the top of the stairs.

Once again Quacky felt around in front of him in the dark. As his hands searched up and down, he felt a handle and gave it a push.

Moonlight filtered down from another small skylight near the ceiling of a room Quacky entered.

"Pattie!" he cried, seeing the dog sitting in the middle of another empty room.

Pattie immediately jumped up on Quacky, her tail wagging, and began licking his hand as he stroked her head.

"She's been all alone in here, crying, I think," Quacky surmised. "I guess this is as far as she could go, pushing against doors and groping around as we've been, in the dark."

Pattie ran to a door and whimpered, then looked back at Quacky anxiously, her tail wagging.

"She wants us to take her through that door," Quacky said, holding back. He had gone through several doors already and so far had not run into anyone. But he was afraid his luck might run out.

"Go ahead, open it," Katie encouraged him, moving up behind Tennis.

Quacky tried hard to keep one happy thought in his mind now. Any door he opened next might lead him to Puddles. He tried not to imagine what else he might find.

The door had a knob on it. So far, he had opened all the other doors just by pushing against them. You couldn't push this one open, he knew: you had to turn the knob to open it. The other doors had been designed for easy access. This was the first one designed to keep people out.

Quacky held the knob and turned it slowly, quietly. He didn't have to tell the others to be as quiet as they could. They knew. And, he was glad to see, so did Pattie.

When he opened the door, Quacky could hardly believe his eyes. A light from a candle on a table in the middle of a small room beyond helped him recognize a familiar face.

"Quacky, what are you doing here?" Morton Horton exclaimed. He was dressed in a bathrobe and his shiny black disco shoes, and he appeared half frightened to death.

"I'm looking for Puddles!" Quacky explained, entering the room with Katie and Tennis crowding behind him. "But I didn't expect to find you! Are your friends here, too?"

The old man looked embarrassed and scratched his chin.

"I might as well confess," Mr. Horton said guiltily.

Are you the dognapper?, Quacky wondered.

Pattie was sitting on the floor at Mr. Horton's side, her tail wagging for some love.

"We heard you tell your Aunt Maggie about Riverland the other day," Mr. Horton explained. "We didn't want to be any trouble to

Maggie, so we decided to come live here. But you've got to get out of here, Quacky. Right away!"

Quacky didn't have time to consider his surprise, to learn that Aunt Maggie's poor old friends were living in Aladdin's Castle because they couldn't afford to buy a condominium. He was too puzzled by Mr. Horton's appearance. The old man was clearly scared about something and wanted them to leave.

"Quick! Go back out the same way you came in!" Mr. Horton said anxiously, turning Quacky around. "Before they see you!"

He pushed Quacky and his pals out of the room and back onto the stair landing, but Quacky had some questions to ask.

"Why do we have to go?" Quacky asked. "Who are 'they'?"

"Never mind, just get out of the castle, right away!" Mister Horton closed the door behind them and called to them from inside the room: "Be careful. And bring the police back with you!"

"I bet the dognappers are hiding out here!" Quacky told Katie and Tennis. "We'd better go for the police now, for sure! Pattie? Pattie, where are you?"

The stairwell was pitch dark again as they started down the creaky old wooden stairs.

"She must have stayed up there, with that

old man," Katie said. "Want to go back up for her?"

"*I've* got to!" Quacky told them, turning around on the stairs and reaching out for the door again. "But you two go back out through the tunnel. And tell Ralph and Will to ride their bikes as fast as they can and bring the police back here. Then how about you two coming back up here, for me and Pattie?"

Katie and Tennis agreed to his plan and started back down the stairs in the dark. Before they reached the bottom, Quacky called out to them from the door at the top of the stairs:

"Go back to the dungeon and out of the castle through the tunnel, like you showed me, Tennis. It's still the fastest way out I know."

Quacky turned the doorknob again and burst into the small room where he had left Pattie and Mister Horton. But neither of them was there.

DEL ROBLE SCHOOL LIBRARY

13

UNDER
A FULL MOON

The room he was in puzzled Quacky. It didn't look like the other rooms in the castle. It had a cot and a cupboard besides the table with the lighted candle on it, and it looked more like a room to live in. There was nothing in it to frighten visitors to Aladdin's Castle.

Maybe it was the caretaker's room, he thought as he noticed another door in the room. It was unlocked, and as Quacky stepped through, he guessed Mister Horton and Pattie had gone through it and into the next room.

The room was empty. It had a very high ceiling and skylight. It was the brightest room Quacky had been in so far. And the scariest.

Skulls hung from ropes and chains on the

walls and ceiling. Pirate ships were painted on the walls, and old bones lay on the floor. He was disappointed to find that Mister Horton wasn't there. Neither was Pattie.

Just then, Quacky was startled when a hand reached out from behind and closed over his mouth. Almost in the same instant, he was roughly lifted off the floor. Someone held him by his shoulders while someone else took his legs.

Quacky was turned upside down so he could see only the floor. The person who held him by the arms and chest managed to keep Quacky's head pushed straight down, so he could not look up or around.

He tried biting the hand that held his head down, but could not reach that far, even though he squirmed and twisted as they held him tightly and started to walk away with him.

"Bet he didn't come alone!" Quacky heard a man's voice say gruffly.

"Don't matter. We'll take care of *him*, same as we're gonna take care of the old geezers!" another man snarled.

They're the dognappers, and they're going to take care of me, the same as they're going to take care of Mister Horton and Aunt Maggie's other old friends, Quacky thought, frightened. He wondered what the two meant by "take care" of them.

"Pattie!" he managed to cry out. "Puddles! Help!"

"He's calling to his pals," one of the men growled. "Well, nobody's gonna help him, are they?"

The other man did not answer as he held the top half of Quacky.

"That's all we needed, one *more!*" the man holding Quacky's legs said, as Quacky was carried up some stairs. "We're gonna have to find ourselves a new hiding place. Why'd those old-timers have to pick our nice hideout?"

"It's that old guy's fault, I bet," the man in front replied. "He seems to know the kid."

Quacky figured they meant Morton Horton.

"Hey, I can walk!" Quacky insisted, struggling to move his legs. "Why not let me loose, and I can walk where you want to take me?"

"No way!" the man in front growled. "A squirmy kid like you can get loose faster than some of these dogs and cats around here."

"Puddles!" Quacky shouted again. He wriggled harder to free himself as the two men carried him up some stairs to what he imagined was the top floor of the old castle. He called out again to Puddles, louder. He began hearing lots of dogs barking ahead of him somewhere. But if Puddles was anywhere around, Quacky could not recognize his bark.

Just as the men carried him into a room at

the top of the stairs, Quacky saw dogs and cats coming at them from every direction, barking and crying, snarling and spitting, at his two captors.

"Puddles!" Quacky called again.

He heard a mean growl and snarl close by but he couldn't see the dog that seemed more upset than all the others.

"Oh, no!" the man holding Quacky's legs cried. "One of the mutts is *his!*" He dropped Quacky, throwing up his hands as he ran.

Quacky got to his knees on the floor and held out his arms. A dark brown Labrador retriever with one white paw and a white streak on his neck began running toward Quacky.

As Quacky saw the two men run out through an open door with an army of dogs and cats chasing after them, Puddles jumped on Quacky and knocked him over.

"We can't let them get away!" he told Puddles, happy as he was to find him.

He stumbled to his feet but found he couldn't move until he got rid of the pillow that was stuck somewhere inside his turtleneck sweater and his jeans.

"Where's Pattie?" Quacky asked as he and Puddles ran through the open door and into a hallway.

Puddles padded ahead, and Quacky figured he was taking him to Pattie. Quacky began sneezing in sixes and knew it was because of all the cats around them. He figured Jennifer-Louise was among them.

"I've got to bring Pattie and Jennifer-Louise back, safe and sound," Quacky told Puddles. He saw that Puddles had stopped at another door and was whining.

"This spook-house and its doors!" Quacky wailed. "It's getting so, I'm afraid to open another one!"

This door had no knob or handle on it. Quacky leaned his shoulder against it, and Puddles helped by leaping up and pushing against it with his two front paws.

Down, down, down, they slid!

They fell so far and fast, down a dark, winding wooden slide, that Quacky thought they must be going all the way down to the basement of the castle again. But when his feet touched ground and Puddles tumbled over onto him, Quacky looked up and saw Felix Morgnester staring at him, bewildered. They were outside the castle!

"They went *that* way!" Felix exclaimed, pointing.

Now Quacky could see and hear them. A whole pack of dogs and cats was chasing the two dognappers out onto the midway.

"You'll never catch them!" someone said to Quacky.

Quacky turned and saw Morton Horton, in his bathrobe and disco shoes. Behind him, also in nightclothes, were Midge Cooper, Ella Grately, and Frank Norton.

"I'm gonna try!" Quacky shouted, hardly able to comprehend what was going on. "Come on, Puddles! We've got work to do!"

Up ahead he saw Pattie. She was trying hard to lead the tangle of dogs and cats on the heels of the two dognappers. Puddles took off from his master's side and raced to catch up with Pattie.

Quacky had never heard so much barking and squealing and crying and snarling and spitting as the dogs and cats pursued the two frantic men up the midway.

After only a few minutes, he heard someone calling his name. Looking behind as he ran, he saw Katie Nolan and Tennis Harper sprinting after him. They must have climbed up to the top floor of the castle and then slid down the slide after me, Quacky thought.

Just before Quacky could catch up with the dognappers and the menagerie chasing them, the two men leaped over a low turnstile. They started running up a tilting platform alongside the roller-coaster tracks. The iron tracks on a wooden structure towered high up over the amusement park.

Quacky jumped the stile just as Puddles and

Pattie raced under it, and he almost came down on top of them as he landed. They three led the pack of dogs and cats up the platform.

When the two men reached the end of the platform, they took a quick look behind them. Seeing all the dogs and cats on their heels, they jumped off the platform and began climbing the roller-coaster tracks, up into the sky.

The furious animals started up the tracks as best they could, but the cats outdid the dogs, with their ability to jump and grasp with their claws. The two dognappers had to keep climbing higher up the tracks, hand over foot, to keep ahead of the leaping cats spitting after them and the dogs barking and snarling behind the cats.

Puddles and Pattie stopped at the edge of the platform with Quacky. They watched, barking loudly, as the dognappers kept mounting higher to escape their pursuers.

Shortly after, Katie and Tennis ran up, and Quacky pointed to the top of the first high climb of the roller coaster, about as tall as an eight-story building. The dogs had stopped a short way below the peak, but remained on the tracks, barking and growling. The cats were up higher, spitting and trying to claw at the dognappers.

Felix Morgnester and the other old folks caught up with Quacky and his pals. They stood below the roller-coaster tracks with them and watched.

Over the barking and spitting, Quacky heard the wail of a police siren. Toward the front of the abandoned amusement park, far up the deserted midway under the glow of the full moon, Quacky saw at least half a dozen speeding squad cars.

A few minutes later, as the cars came to screeching stops just below the roller coaster, Quacky saw a witch and a magician step quickly out of one of the police cars and run toward him.

"Quacky, what's going on?" Aunt Maggie asked excitedly, waving her long thin arms still covered with long black gloves.

Right behind Jerry in his black magician's suit, Quacky saw Lieutenant Sally O'Rourke and Chief of Police Dooley. Rushing up behind them were Spiderman and a ghost in a sheet.

Aunt Maggie had no sooner satisfied herself that Quacky was safe and that Puddles was back with him at last, than she saw her old friends standing on the roller-coaster platform, shivering in their robes and nightgowns.

"We heard Quacky tell about Aladdin's Castle," Midge Cooper began to explain to her. "We thought maybe we'd take up residence there, rent free."

"It was all right, too," Ella Grately added.

"Until we found we had fallen into a den of
dog-and-catnappers!"

"When Quacky paid his surprise visit, Puddles took over and routed the dognappers!"
Frank Norton said, picking up the story.

"They were going to hold us for ransom,
too!" Morton Horton put in. "I had a devil of a
time, keeping them from stealing my disco
shoes!"

"They're my shoes!" Frank Norton insisted.
This time, he was ignored.

"I knew the dognappers were hiding out
here," Felix admitted. "But they threatened
they would 'take care of me,' if I snitched to
the police."

Quacky had a mental picture of all the old
folks being stretched out on the medieval torture rack in the dungeon, one by one.

Puddles and Pattie came away from the
roller-coaster tracks and began wagging their
tails and looking for love from Quacky as half
a dozen policemen began climbing up the
tracks. The dogs and cats were retrieved, but
they kept on barking or spitting.

Finally, the two dognappers were brought
down from high atop the roller-coaster tracks,
and handcuffed.

"Good work, Quacky," Lieutenant O'Rourke
told him, and Quacky was glad. He could tell
by looking at Jerry that he thought everything
was okay, too.

"I had a hunch you'd wind up here tonight," Jerry told Quacky. "If Aunt Maggie and I could have explained everything to the police sooner, we'd have been here before this. I guess I should have just let you handle everything in the first place."

"But I'm afraid you folks can't go back living here in Riverland," Chief Dooley warned Felix and the other oldsters. "It's closed down and could be dangerous."

"What do you mean, '*could be*'!" Ella Grately declared, wrapping her robe closer around her to keep warm.

"They'll all be coming home with Quacky and Jerry and me," Aunt Maggie assured the police chief, hugging her lady friends.

"Not for a permanent stay though, Maggie," Morton Horton told her.

"But it sure will be a relief, to go back to your place, Maggie, after what we've been through in Aladdin's Castle!" Midge Cooper said, shivering in the cold night air. "The only good thing about it was, I found Felix again!"

Quacky remembered that Felix Morgnester and Miss Cooper had known each other years ago, at the pavilion in the park.

A cold wind blew across the midway. Everyone looked up to see dark storm clouds begin to pass over the full moon. Quacky half expected to see a witch on a broomstick flying across it.

"I told you, Quacky," Aunt Maggie said, putting an arm around him. "Weird things go on, under a full moon!"

As Quacky reached down to pat both Puddles and Pattie, he saw a bedraggled white kitten with a pink nose coming toward him, crying. A red-silk ribbon was tied around its neck, and a long length of ribbon trailed behind. .

Quacky began to sneeze. Six times.

14

ONE LAST STRAY

"Which one of you wants to report first?" Miss Irmgaard Effie asked her Social Studies class on Monday afternoon.

Quacky was looking out the window. The sun was shining, and Puddles was waiting for him under a tree. He didn't even have to be leashed. Quacky knew Puddles would wait for him through an earthquake, since they had been reunited. Unless the "call of the wild" sounded, he thought, and Puddles would run off to pay Pattie another visit.

"Quacky, how about you?" Miss Effie addressed him, shaking him out of his latest daydream of playing with Puddles. "The

Smedley Gazette is only a weekly paper and won't come out until Thursday. I'm sure the rest of the class is as interested as I am to hear your report on Riverland. And not only its history, but what went on there just last night!"

"Well, I never did get to look up any newspaper or library clippings about Riverland," Quacky admitted. "Things just happened too fast. But I learned a lot about it, from Felix Morgnester, who used to be the best carnival barker on the midway."

Tennis looked at Quacky and didn't mind that he was making the report for them both.

"Riverland goes back to about 1924," Quacky began. "Amusement parks like it were once very popular around the country. Especially after the big stock-market crash in 1929. I guess lots of people were out of work and didn't have much money. But they needed a place to go where they could laugh and have fun and forget their troubles.

"Felix Morgnester says he started working there in 1934, singing in the pavilion. He says he was a hit singing a song called 'When Yuba Plays the Rumba on the Tuba'."

Quacky couldn't go on with his story until the laughs stopped.

"But when he heard a soprano named Midge Cooper sing some opera there one night, he gave up singing and became a midway barker. He says her singing gave him the idea."

More laughs filled the room before he could continue.

"Now they're both staying at my Aunt Maggie's house, and from the way they're carrying on, I think, if you listen closely, in a couple of weeks you're gonna hear wedding bells."

Some of his louder classmates began whistling and clapping.

"I guess what Riverland amounted to was, it was a fun place to go. I've never been to Disneyland, but I guess it's like Riverland used to be, only bigger.

"People need to see something that scares or excites them, like spook-houses and roller coasters," Quacky surmised. "And fun houses where they can laugh at things. Some doctor, my Aunt Maggie told me, says that 'laughter is the best medicine'."

Then Quacky told them what happened on Halloween night at Riverland, and the other kids applauded when he finished.

"I guess I don't have much more to say about Riverland," Quacky concluded. "Except that somewhere along the way, it died. Some folks say people began staying away when television became popular. But last night, Mister MacDougall, the president of the First National Bank of Smedley, says he's going to talk to some big businessmen in town. He says he thinks we need Riverland again, to help people have fun again and take their minds off inflation and the mess the world's in. He thinks they can come up with enough money to re-open Riverland."

That got Quacky the biggest hand of all.

He wanted to go out and play with Puddles in the worst way, but he knew he had to wait until the end of the hour, after some of the others gave their class reports.

But when he looked up at the clock, Quacky discovered it was just a few minutes before three. He had talked longer then he realized.

"Thank you, Quacky," Miss Effie told him. "That was a very fine report. Class dismissed!"

Quacky ran out of the classroom and down the hall. When he got outside, he stopped short of the tree where he had left Puddles.

"He's *gone!*" Quacky cried, looking at Tennis and Ralph, who had just joined him.

"Don't worry, Quacky," Tennis assured him. "This time, I don't suppose it was dognappers, do you?"

Quacky only had to think for a moment.

"No, I guess I know where he went!"

Quacky ran for his bike and his pals got theirs and followed him, riding over to Mattie Mayflower's house.

They found Puddles romping on Mattie's front lawn with Pattie. It was a warm afternoon, and Miss Mayflower was sitting outside with Aunt Maggie and all her old friends, having some tea and sunshine.

"Quacky, I've wonderful news!" Aunt Maggie called to him as he and his friends came into the yard.

He was going to ask if his aunt had found Uncle Otis again, but decided not to bring it up, in case he was still among the missing.

"Midge Cooper's going to be Miss Mayflower's nurse," Aunt Maggie told him excitedly. "And she and Mister Morgnester and my other friends are all going to live here, with Miss Mayflower."

"Of course, we're all going to pitch in and fix it up, with some fresh paint and furnish it nice again," Felix added.

"It's too big a house for just me," Mattie Mayflower said, and Quacky thought she looked a lot better and happier. "I was just rattling around in it, like an old skeleton. Now, thank heaven, I'll have some company. But I'm sure we wouldn't all have gotten together, except for you, Quacky."

It all makes good sense, Quacky thought. They all need each other. Why not get together?

"What are you going to do with the $500 reward money for helping find Mrs. MacDougall's cat?" Miss Mayflower asked Quacky.

Quacky had been thinking about that and looked at Aunt Maggie.

"I think all of you folks really found Jennifer-Louise, before I did," Quacky told them.

"So the reward money is yours, to split among you."

He knew, from what Aunt Maggie had told him, that $500 to the old folks would look like $5,000, they needed help so badly. It took a while, but Quacky let himself be talked into taking one share of the reward money. He wasn't exactly sure what $500 split six ways would come to. Less than $100, he knew. But he would find a good way to spend as much as he would get.

And Quacky also knew he was going to be making a little extra spending money for a while. Mrs. MacDougall had forgiven him for losing her cat and, when she asked him, Quacky agreed to walk Jennifer-Louise on her leash again every day. He just said the cat would have to get used to walking before or after school.

A police car drove up to the front of the Mayflower house. Quacky saw Jerry get out with Lieutenant O'Rourke, who was in her blue police uniform.

"Hello!" Lieutenant O'Rourke called to them. "I see you're all resting a little, after your busy night."

Quacky still couldn't quite get used to her being a cop. Every time she came by, he was afraid she was coming to arrest him for something. But even so, he found that he liked her more every time she came around. Maybe it was because Jerry seemed to like her more all the time.

Aunt Maggie told Jerry and Sally the news that her friends would be all living with Miss Mayflower.

"And, Quacky," Miss Mayflower called to him. "There's something else you ought to know. I talked with the veterinarian this morning, about Pattie. She's been acting a little strangely lately, and he told me why. She's in a family way!"

Quacky looked at Puddles, and it made sense. Puddles was playing more gently with Pattie than usual. He knows, Quacky figured, that some day not too far off, she's going to be a mother.

"We've come over with some news of our own," Jerry told everyone. "Quacky, I would have told you first, but I guess this is as good a time as any to tell you and Aunt Maggie. Sally and I are going to be married."

Quacky was sort of expecting something like that, but hearing Jerry say it was a surprise, almost a shock, to him. But he knew he had been half hoping for the same thing. Looking at Jerry and Sally, Quacky felt sure he knew how things stood among the three of them. He didn't think he was going to lose a potential father, but gain a potential mother!

Before he could say how glad he was, Quacky saw Chief of Police Dooley drive up in his police car. The others looked, too, and just as Quacky saw who it was that Chief Dooley was leading up the walk, Aunt Maggie leaped out of the chair.

"Does this belong to anyone?" Chief Dooley asked, holding the arm of a tall, distinguished-looking gentleman dressed in black slacks and gray sweater. "I found him this afternoon, when I was checking out the dungeon at Aladdin's Castle!"

Aunt Maggie rushed up to the captive and threw her arms around him. "Otis!" she exclaimed happily.

ABOUT THE AUTHOR

Walter Oleksy's first book in the Quacky series was *If I'm Lost, How Come I Found You?* This was followed by *Quacky and the Crazy Curve Ball.* This new book, *Quacky and the Haunted Amusement Park,* like the first book, has been selected by ABC for a television movie. The author's other recent books for teens include *Careers in the Animal Kingdom* and *Women in Men's Jobs.*

A former reporter for *The Chicago Tribune* and past editor of three travel magazines, the author now devotes himself full-time to writing books. For adults, he has written a cookbook, a true adventure story of a canoe trip, and a history of the one-room schoolhouse.

Mr. Oleksy enjoys camping, wilderness canoeing, gardening, and "anything outdoors." He and his dog Chelsea live in Evanston, Illinois.